I0689095

Fiction's Fall

Fiction's Fall

Morgan A. Colbert

Copyright © 2023 by Morgan A. Colbert

All rights reserved. No part of this book may be reproduced in any manner whatsoever without written permission except in the case of brief quotations embodied in critical articles and reviews.

First Printing, 2025

Austin, TX

ISBN: 979-8-9924049-0-6

Library of Congress Control Number: 2025900809

Cover image created with Canva

Cover layout created with Ingram Sparks

CONTENTS

For my dad, who kindly haunts these pages.

SUNDAY, BUT NOT YET SUNDAY

Families lie to one another. It's a fact; they become so good at it. They learn each other's tells as if life was a game of cards. They grow up discovering secrets, building fictions, stretching their imaginations, and simultaneously exploring and exploiting each other's weaknesses. When it comes to familial deception, it's hard to place the blame and know whether it's your fault or theirs. And so, with all of this said and held as an almost cosmic belief, I really shouldn't have been shocked by what my cousin Brynn said on that Saturday night. Well, actually, early Sunday morning.

"Lynman, you know Abe's your dad, right?" she said while sprawled across the old floral print couch.

"Huh?" It would be a couple seconds until I caught up with her, as the couch was my present focus. I was busy pondering the colors and swirls of pattern, debating on why the couch hadn't been thrown out years ago. It had holes and rips, and looked fit for an alley or abandoned house, but it was still comfy enough to prove the best place for a nap any day. That night it would be my bed, though truthfully, I could have slept heaped on a staircase in my present state. It was past three in the morning and the apartment was obscenely lit for that time of night, but it didn't matter. Nothing mattered. We were as high as a couple of kites. I was so high, I kept laughing and staring at my hands as if they were perfect and magical. It was always the same. And really, I hate smoking pot and never do so if I can help it. Brynn being my big exception; well, Brynn and Llew, but my West Coast brother didn't come east often enough to make it a regular occurrence.

Brynn is one of those creatures who seems to operate most of her day under the influence. She works, runs errands, enjoys hobbies, cooks the best fucking chocolate chip cookies I've ever had; all while completely blitzed out of her mind.

I'm the opposite, and more traditional in my vices. I try to stick with cigarettes and alcohol. After a little bit of weed, I can focus on everything or nothing. I'm entranced with whatever crosses my path. I'm as hungry as a fourteen-year-old boy, and paranoid as all fuck. Oh, and I cuss a lot. But the very worst part, in my personal opinion, is the fact that I have a traumatizing relationship with horror movies when I'm high.

I don't know why people always want to watch horror movies. I mean, they're alright when I'm in the right mindset, and by that I mean I've found a perfectly good way of hiding behind the collar of my shirt and daydreaming myself away from what's happening on the screen. Unfortunately, that's just not an option when I'm high. Any horror movie becomes the scariest thing on Earth. I realistically accept all the setups and bad storylines as true to life. I cried once during this French thriller about a serial killer. Yet the thing that really matters, what makes it stand out, is the fact that I remember; well, sort of remember.

You see, I rarely recall any part of those high nights. It's the mix of the pot with the booze, but the one thing always seems to follow the other and I wake up in a fogged out cloud. Usually I just remember how I feel. I recall being happy, or feeling paranoid. But after a horror movie, my whole body is sick. I feel the terror in my muscles, in my heart. It messes up the whole next day. It's definitely not worth it, so if I can help it I don't smoke, and if Brynn's peer pressure gets too heavy then I'll make sure we're in for the night; safely locked away in her apartment surrounded by pizza, ice cream, and completely forgettable rom-coms. I know well and good that this is an event I'll just need to write off, though I've gotten into the habit of interrogating Brynn over the coming days if I'm too concerned about what may have transpired. For example, this whole story I'm telling you now came together in pieces later on, but for the sake of storytelling, you and I are going to take a different and more knowing view.

"Emlyn," she said, calling me by my proper name to get my attention before repeating, "you know Abe's your dad, right?"

I flinched at my name, since there are very few people who are allowed to use it, and not even my dear cousin Brynn was one of them.

I sighed dramatically before echoing what she had said, "Abe's my dad."

Once the sentence sank in I started to laugh and in turn, so did she. I fell over in a heap next to the couch and she rolled off onto the floor with a hard thump, which made it all even funnier. Somewhere below you could hear someone striking the cciling in the hopes of shutting us up, and we drew our hands over our mouths to flail a bit more quietly.

"Abe's my dad," I said rather than asked, catching a glimpse of my hands and turning them over in front of my eyes. "Abraham Newman, my father," I repeated. The words were becoming comfortable, my ears took in the sound, my mouth the truth and the embrace of my own last name. "I wonder why they never told me? Why didn't you tell me?"

"Dad made me promise. Lynman, you can't say anything, alright?" She looked up afraid for a moment and sniffed the air before running across the apartment to pull the cookies out of the oven.

The thought of her burning the cookies, or worse, the building down around us, made me terrified for a second. I felt a wave of dread.

"Who's the woman, well my, the mom?" I stumbled over the words as my brain stumbled over the knowledge, unsure what to say or how to say it.

Brynn shrugged, hardly listening as she shifted cookies onto a plate for us to devour. She tossed a wave of blond hair back over her shoulder. The motion was enough to almost steal my attention, but she kept talking and I stayed focused. "Just some girl from Dash, that boarding school he went to in Vermont. They got knocked up when they were both like fifteen. It must have been his experimental phase," said Brynn, waving it all away along with the heat coming off the cookies, since Abe's gay.

"Just some girl," I repeated painfully to myself.

Not hearing me, Brynn laughed some more and carried the plate back into the living room, setting it down on the coffee table.

"Jesus, I'm tired. Why the fuck are all these lights on?" She laughed again, a rolling sound followed her as she flipped most the switches off.

"I'm not going to remember any of this in the morning," I said defeated, and wedged almost an entire cookie in my mouth. "Do you have any milk? I'm going to get some milk," I said, or maybe just tried to say behind a mouthful of chocolate goodness before standing up and crossing the room.

"That's why I told you. Wait, what did you ask?"

I swallowed hard. "Milk?"

"Yeah, well, the almond type. This way you won't remember, and so it doesn't really matter if I tell you or not. I'm going to bed. I have to wake up early, but stay however long you want. Just lock the door behind you when you go."

"Cool, cool."

"Eat the cookies," Brynn said and disappeared. The bedroom door closed and I was alone.

"Night," I said quietly to no one in particular.

I stood there, swaying slightly, staring intently at the oven for a few moments making sure it was actually turned off. The room had grown almost unbearably quiet, but my heart was racing, drumming in my ears. Finally, I remembered the milk and poured a tall glass that I drank slowly while staring into the fridge with its quilt of colors and shapes. Slowly, I closed the door but my eyes stayed busy, staring at a collection of magnets, wedding announcements and baby invitations. A shopping list was hanging there with way too much information to make out.

Who would have thought the words Ziploc bags, shampoo, and pasta would be so confusing, but it certainly was in that moment.

Thoughtlessly, I tore the bottom of the list free and grabbed the pen that hung there. I scribbled those words that I knew I would forget, but sober me needed something to explain the new feeling that would show up in the morning.

*Abe's your dad. He **knocked** up some Dashell girl!*

And there you have it, that's how I learned that my brother was really my father.

THE LIE

I woke up the next morning face first into the couch, my arm and cheek pretty well drool-covered and imprinted with the texture of the sofa. I was sweaty and gross, while the taste in my mouth was dry and horrible. Groaning, I stretched, flipping over on my back and wiping the ick away. The apartment was quiet, but down below in the Astoria, Queens streets, the sound of the day was in full swing. Checking my phone, I realized it was nearly noon. Things were moving hideously fast. I had to work that evening and I knew I needed to get going.

There was a cookie on the table and I shoved it in my mouth. What I really wanted to do was fall back asleep, but instead I slipped on my shoes, and with that, was pretty much ready to walk out the door, but first I thought I would pee and see if there was any mouthwash to help put out the dumpster fire burning out of control on my tastebuds. I tried to remember the night before. It was generally a blank, bleary vision of my hands and the knowledge that we had laughed a great deal. At least my core felt the chuckles; it was as if I'd done a couple dozen sit-ups. To me, that felt like an alright time with Brynn, though I was disappointed that I let myself get talked into smoking and in turn losing the hours both last night and that morning which I'd slept away.

I glanced in the mirror by the front door and realized I looked old. Shoot, I felt old. I was only twenty-seven, but my brown hair was going light, well, probably gray, though to me it looked like it was covered in a layer of dust and that didn't help me cling to my idea of youth. I ran my hands through it and pulled it away from my face into a tight ponytail.

I'd recently lost a bit of weight, not a whole lot, maybe fifteen pounds. Work had been keeping me busy, and I didn't have as much time to sit around, drink, or get high and eat cookies like I used to; it's for the best.

My sister keeps commenting on the weight, which is nice to hear, but my clothes don't seem to fit as well anymore. Something else my sister likes to comment on... it's always one thing or another with her. I took a deep breath, avoiding my eyes in the mirror and mentally gave myself the old talking to. I needed to try and not do this anymore. I needed to get my life in order. I'd heard them all say it, Mom, Dad, Medi, even Llew. And Llewelyn could be an idiot. The only person who didn't harp on me was my oldest brother Abraham. Old, dependable Abe. He used to say, 'you'll get there when you get there.' It was something I've always sort of held on to, like a mantra.

Right now, what I needed was to get home and take a shower. With a sigh, I turned toward the door. I tapped my bag and checked my pockets for my keys and phone. Sticking my hand in my back pocket I pulled out an odd scrap of paper. I got excited thinking it was cash for a minute, but it wasn't. Yet it was too heavy to be a receipt either, so I unfolded it and squinted at the words.

*Abe's your dad. He **<u>knocked</u>** up some Dashell girl!*

I paused, and everything stopped for a minute. I just took it all in, I had to, letting the words unravel, parsing whatever this was. Trying to remember why I had it, and where it had come from. It was as if I'd written a joke to play on myself, but it didn't feel that way. I frowned, noticing I had underlined and traced over the word 'knocked.' That was where the joke was, the word, not the meaning. I managed an odd snort of laughter before letting my thoughts settle.

Oddly enough, quickly enough, I accepted it as true. Maybe it was because I recognized my handwriting, but there was no shock in this announcement. It was almost like I should have known, maybe I'd always known and somehow just forgotten, and this was the reminder. But that wasn't right either. I mean, I knew my parents weren't my biological parents. I knew I was adopted. I found out when I was about nine. It was on Llew's birthday actually, he was the one turning nine. I was still eight and I would be for the next few months. Growing up, I always thought Llew and I were twins. It wasn't until the year before, when someone explained that generally you had to share the same birthday to be twins. It took a while and a lot of questions from me to realize it was hardly possible to be twins three months apart, and then the bewilderment accumulated to about a week prior when this girl in my class, Heather Spinner, explained a bit more about the magic of babies and how they had an approximate baking timeline of about nine months. So on that day sitting around the birthday cake and thinking about my family really nothing made sense.

There we were. Llew had just blown out the candles. Mom was cutting the cake and the room was a bustle, full of noise and happiness. And I busted it all up, asked the question about this wobbly timeline. As soon as the words were uttered, the silence was all you felt, folks staring nowhere, nobody wanting to look at one person for too long, well everyone except Abe. I do remember him looking only at me. He never faltered and it looked like he was on the verge of saying something, but instead Mom took charge. That's what Mom does, always has. She took charge and just said, with total nonchalance, as if I were dumb because I hadn't already known, as if this was something that's ingrained inside, that truth about how a person fits inside their family.

"You're adopted, and that's why you and Llew are so close in age."

There you have it.

"Oh," I remember saying with a frown and now everyone looked at me. Dad kept opening and closing his mouth, looking at Mom like he wanted to take something back or disagree with her, but he couldn't and finally it was Llew who broke the silence pointing at me and doing one of his big Nelson, from *The Simpsons* laughs. Dad reached out and slapped him on the back of the head and Mom started serving cake like nothing had happened. And that was the end of it. After a moment I got up, mumbling something about a glass of water and proceeded to walk out the door.

I remember passing by Medi and Henry on the sidewalk. The two of them arrived late, and my sister asked, "Did we miss cake?"

I responded, "Did you know I'm adopted?"

The two of them joined the silent staring club and I crossed the street to our town's cemetery and climbed up to the morbidly placed playground at the top of the hill. That's where I stayed until Henry showed up with a piece of cake. Silently we did some swinging and eating, and then walked home together.

I kept running this story through my mind as I drove home. I was on the old motorcycle my parents both hate and the ride was much too automatic for my liking. My hands knew the controls, my brain knew the path, but that wasn't good enough. I'm really not comfortable on the motorcycle unless I feel completely involved with every task. It's easy to know why my parents hate the thing, but I can't help it. I love it entirely. It's like electricity and poetry all folded into one. The way it flows and moves through me, under me, all around me. I guess I'm just smart enough to know I'm an idiot for keeping it around.

I'm staying with my parents right now after having graduated with my master's degree last year. Since then, I've been working at the library. It seems, I collect degrees like other people collect nice purses or comic books. I just keep thinking I know what I want but then I get it, and realize there must have been a mistake along the way. Anyway, my parents seem really happy that I'm staying with them. Everyone else has moved away.

Sure, my folks are getting older, but they've hardly slowed down. Dad had a bit of a break recently because of a health scare. He had a heart attack about six months ago. It was pretty terrifying, but he's better now. It was good because it forced him to take a vacation from his shop. And Mom, she's got her art. She's locked away all day long and most of the night painting. If she's not painting, she's taking part in shows, traveling around the country, and lecturing. I suppose she's a real success, though being an accomplished artist isn't really the same as being an actor or a musician. People buy her art and keep it locked away. She might be on a page in a modern textbook, but unless you yourself are an artist or a collector or live in our town, you'd have no idea who she is, but she was the real money in the family. We all knew it. We knew it because she was always so carefree, and my Dad with the bookstore was the opposite.

When I close my eyes and picture my dad, I see him at the kitchen table surrounded by bills. I see him hunched over and silent. I see all of us kids slinking from room to room so he might not link whatever bad news he's considering to one of us.

Now, back to the moment at hand. After roaring down the lane, I arrived home, and parked my bike on the edge of the driveway before sneaking in the front door and quietly heading upstairs. The house seemed peaceful and vacant but it's Sunday and I couldn't think where else my parents would be. I just slipped off my shoes and slid on socks making the house feel giant, and trying to empty my mind.

I took a shower and that helped; my hands doing more than anything else to calm me down. I cleared my mind. I wasted hot water and didn't give it much concern because my parents lied to me my whole life.

I was feeling better once I was dressed in clean clothes, and had brushed my teeth. It's amazing how much toothpaste can reinvigorate a mood. The house wasn't as quiet now. I could hear the little TV in the kitchen. I probably should have just left, taken more time alone to consider what I might or might not do with this new information. If I was going to take my anger out on someone it might be better to do so on strangers. It probably wasn't a good idea to see someone I was trying to come to terms with having lied to me every day for the last 27 years, but I wasn't thinking cautiously at that hour and so I wandered in the kitchen to see Dad sitting over a bowl of tomato soup. He's pretty much the only person I know who eats tomato soup. Well we all did growing up, but for some reason the rest of us stopped.

"Hey Dad."

He looked small sitting there with his soup. Wearing fingerless gloves because he's always cold, in a sweatshirt that's as old as me, and with his silvery yet somehow dark hair combed perfectly in place. He was watching *The Great Escape*. It's a movie we both love. He didn't respond when I spoke because Steve McQueen, James Garner and another American POW are all making moonshine and I know it's his favorite scene. The characters march out to celebrate the 4th of July, and I glanced back to smile at Dad, but I realize he's not smiling, or watching the screen. He's looking at me.

"What's up?"

"You got some mail," he said and reached across the small kitchen table to grab a thick envelope. The logo in the corner read UCLA. I could tell the envelope had been opened by the way it sat a bit wonky.

"What's it say?"

"So you're going back to school? Emlyn, do you have any idea how much an out of state school like UCLA is going to cost you?" To my real surprise he looked angry.

"Oh, so I guess I got in, that's nice." I waved him off. "Don't worry about the money. You're not the one who's going to have to pay for it. Besides, Llew and I spoke, I'll use his address, and work it out."

He forcibly pointed first at me and then at the envelope pinning the paper down. "It's nice you've given this so much thought, you and your brother both, and never in all of this did you think of telling your mother or I."

"Jesus Dad, it's not set in stone. It was just an idea. Shit, why are you so upset? It's cheaper than a kid, or a house, or any number of things I could be spending money on. Me going back to school is not the worst thing that could happen."

He threw up his hands and I just had no idea why he was so angry, and then it came. "Your mother and I were depending on you. She's going to need you around here. We're going to need you to help with the store."

"Dad-"

"I'm sick kiddo," he said.

It wasn't the type of thing I was expecting. I don't think he was expecting it either, he waved the words away making the same gesture I had made a moment before and I shook my head not believing him. Thinking this was a cheap trick there to manipulate me.

"Oh, come off of it Dad, you're not sick. You're better now. You're mowing the fucking lawn-"

"Mouth," he said sternly as if I'm thirteen again.

I kept going, "and walking to the post office every day. You and Mom will be fine. You've got Medi just one town over. You know I don't appreciate you making this shit up."

"Hey!" he said, his voice rising, "I don't lie to you."

"Really?" I scoffed.

"What the hell is that supposed to mean?" he shouted, and now I was mad too.

I didn't think he had any reason to be the one who was upset. I started to laugh. It was all just too much with what I'd been mulling over all morning. The paper, the bottom half of a shopping list had changed pockets with all the rest of the things that meant to travel my day and so without any real consideration I pulled it free and laid it on top of the envelope from UCLA, the words easy to read between the two of us. The word *knocked* looked nearly grotesque.

Whatever he was planning to say was gone. He just stared at the paper before picking it up. I felt the confirmation in his new found silence. I could have been easily wrong, a bad joke written out of last night's bad decisions, but he didn't know that. This was a truth he hadn't anticipated dealing with that morning. I saw the color drain from his face and realized that his anger at me was gone, and now he seemed both sad and hurt. It's weird, I hadn't considered it would affect him like that and now I was ashamed to see it. I wished I could take it back.

"I'm your father, Emlyn." he whispered.

"I've got to go to work." I stood up with the sudden desire to run, but Dad reached out and grabbed my wrist.

"Lynny," he said more firmly.

"I know Dad," I said, staring at the ground. I realized I was fighting off tears, from where they had come I didn't know. I hadn't invited them. He still had hold of my wrist and pulled me into a hug.

"I love you," he said.

I nodded, shaking my head into his shoulder.

"You too," I finally managed to utter, this was the best he was going to get, I felt the word 'love' in my mouth and knew I couldn't say it. The shape of the word, pushing at my cheek was some sort of a lever, a dam was breaking inside of me and I couldn't control it. I didn't want this to be a thing. I laughed sharply trying to fight tears.

"I think I'm hungover," I sniffed loudly, refusing to look him in the eye. "We'll talk later."

I broke his grip and dashed out of the house.

3

MISCOMMUNICATION

Once I got out of the house and away from Dad I dried up pretty quickly. I looked at my watch and realized I couldn't go to work yet. It was too early and I wasn't going to be caught dead there a second longer than I needed to be. The library wasn't far from our house. So I went the long way toward a local coffee shop. It was maybe a mile walk. It was nice out, a beautiful fall day, but I had a hard time enjoying it. When I reached my detour, I'm sure it looked like I was fighting allergies and I leaned into the act, with a false cough into my elbow. I ordered a pesto grilled cheese and an iced coffee, and once I was sitting on the empty back porch, called Medi.

I have a weird relationship with my eldest siblings. At least I imagine it's strange, mostly because of the age difference. Abe's 43, Medi is 39 and Llew and I are both 27. So they were both starting to live outside of the house around the time I was forming real solid memories. Medi loves to mother me. She loves to make these statements about what it's like to be an adult. She tries to tell me how much I should tip at restaurants, as if I learned to count yesterday. She lectures on how the purchase of furniture is one of the keys to growing up. She drives me crazy, but one of the real great things about her is that she's a good person to complain with. She answered the phone in mid complaint about Mom and I felt instantly at ease. This is why I called her.

"That's the last time I take Mom shopping," she said as a way of a hello.

I was on speakerphone and I could tell she had answered while driving. I hate when I'm on speakerphone and I hate that she uses the phone when she drives, but since I had called her I didn't feel like I could say goodbye just yet, not without her knowing the reason for the quick turn around and thus opening the door for a new argument. So instead, I hello back with, "yeah, what did she do?"

"I have no idea where this sunglasses phase came from. She's acting like Bennie is Stevie Wonder. And the money she wants to spend on this stuff. He'll be lucky not to lose them in the first week and then we'll all enjoy that story for the rest of our lives about how Bennie lost a $300 pair of sunglasses. She's impossible."

"That reminds me I need to get him something." The next weekend was my nephew's 17th birthday. Bennie is the most put together 16 year old I've ever met. It probably has a lot to do with his sight. He's not totally blind, but the phrase legally blind is used often. He keeps everything very organized and moves generally slowly and quietly around the room. When he was little he scared the shit out of us any chance he got, sneaking up behind you and shrieking. It made us all laugh, but I think it shaved years off my life.

"You're about the only person I don't worry about when it comes to gifts. You always come up with the best ideas. How do you do it?"

"I was bitten by one of the most boring mutant spiders."

This was about as much of an answer as she was going to get. It's a trap that she was trying to lead me into, because the only reason I'm good at giving gifts is because I listen. I listen when we're watching TV. and someone gets excited about a dumb Infomercial. I listen when someone says what movie they've never seen but really want to. I listen when someone complains that they've lost one glove. It's never interesting gifts, but generally it's what people want. I don't think people ever expect to get what they really want. So maybe it's a nice surprise. Yet, if I was to mention to my sister that listening is the key. All it means, is that she doesn't, which of course is true, but that wasn't the direction this call needed to go.

"That reminds me, Mom was complaining about Llew. He's got some new girlfriend that he has declared to be 'the one.' I think he's known her for maybe a month."

"A love for the ages. I actually think they've been together a bit longer than that."

"You should try and talk to him. You're the only one he listens to," she said half-heartedly.

"Oh yeah, that will go well. I just have so much experience in relationships. I'm the queen of the advice column."

"Well, if you want me to hook you up with the new admin assistant, I'll put in the word. He's cute and up and coming. Get in on the ground floor."

"He's not a start-up, M," I said.

"He is a start-up E, and he wears a tie every day," tossed back Medi.

"I'm out."

"You called me brat, talk soon, love ya." The phone went dead as quick as that.

I hadn't meant I was out of the conversation, only out of the set up, but that was classic for my sister and I, just a world of miscommunication between us. I sighed, but actually felt better about the whole thing. The whole world hadn't changed yet, just a piece of it. As I enjoyed my grilled cheese, part of me just figured I would forget everything. The stuff I learned last night was information for high Lynman, not for regular everyday me. I wasn't expected to remember it, and it was probably for the best. I figured Dad would forget about it as well. So, if that night he gave me a hard time about California, then I would happily accept that he had moved on too. We could just ignore it.

4

HAPPY TROUBLE

Fuck the library. I mean I love the library, it's a giant building filled with books, but I guess I'm one of those dummies that still holds onto the past. When I was a kid we didn't have a dozen computers at the library filled with jerk children shouting about whatever game they played. We had a bunch of kids, terrified of Mrs. Pims, the old librarian. A woman who knew how to scare the silence into you with only a glance. We were all professional whisperers, who gawked over the grossest descriptors in Stephen King novels or that paperback copy of *Jaws* with the naked lady swimming across the cover. I miss mean librarians and quiet. Now the library is a game center filled with entitled children with more rights than I ever had growing up. I spend all day helping cranky old folks figure out how to use their tablets. I get the frustration they carry toward their grown children who bought these bricks as Christmas presents, as we both throw out guesses of their forgotten passwords. It's definitely my own fault, I mean I knew this was what I was getting into. The classes kept teaching me that a public library was about building community bases for neighborhoods, being whatever people need, and this is what my neighborhood seems to need. And I pretty much dislike every single one of these people because of it.

The best thing I can do while at the library is to shelve. It pisses my boss off, because it's stuff the volunteers can do, but at least out among the stacks I can lose myself for a bit. I can hold onto a book, and flip through the pages, full of adventures and stories.

I had a full cart of nonfiction travel books and it took me a long time, not just to shelve them, but to make the oddly sized books straight and tidy. I love keeping the shelves in order. Making sure all of them are in the right place, all making a right angle with the edge of the metal shelf.

I looked at my watch and knew it was almost time for me to go up-front and work the circulation desk. At least the day was winding down. Hooray for Sundays at the library because of these short shifts, everyone works that day, which screws all of us, but it's a shared pain. We all work half a shift, so my oft occurring mix of anxiety and rage usually don't have time to appear before we start closing down.

I was sitting on the foot stool, taking a last deep breath when all of a sudden a tiny map of London fell off one of the higher shelves and hit me squarely on the head. It was a bit of a loud surprise, but thankfully not a painful one. I picked it up and looked for where it had fallen only to see another book begin to slowly edge further out. This one was much bigger and probably would have hurt quite a bit. I looked all around wondering if anyone was close by and seeing what I was seeing, but I was alone. Hopping to my feet and peering below that shelf, I hoped to see someone and grab their attention, but I couldn't see anyone. At least by that time, the book had stopped moving. I sighed loudly in great annoyance, before out of the corner of my eye noticed someone actually was nearby.

It was Henry, glancing at the books around him, trying to appear innocent but at the same time looking guilty as sin. When I caught his eye he relaxed and stood there leaning, it was a good lean. Jesus, he was a good leaner. A straight body that made the best angles with shelves that I had ever seen. The man was pure geometry. There was almost always a turned up corner of his shirt, showing flat, tan skin above his belt. It was something I had come to expect and had trained myself not to stare at like I wanted to.

"You know, I could ask you to leave for messing with the collection in such a disrespectful manner. I had to tell off a 13 year-old just the other day for doing practically the same thing."

"I have no idea what you're talking about. I just got here," said Henry, unconcerned while at the same time flashing his crooked smile.

I looked away, knowing I would have a stupid grin to match his. Sometimes looking at him I would smile too much, like I had won the lottery instead of just taking part in a normal person to person conversation. He was dangerous to be around.

"What's up?" I asked, ignoring his perfect form and finding the place from which London had fallen and setting it right.

"Just passing by, hoping I might catch you," he responded.

"Just passing by? Really, Hank dear? You got the look of one with information to spend," I realized my voice was sounding weird and a bit twangy, while in my head I was writing dialogue for the cool lead, which wasn't exactly my credit. I glanced back at Henry and to great annoyance he winked and my face hurt from trying to tame my grin. I shook my head and started lining up books again, making already straight books straighter.

"What are you doing Thursday night?" asked Henry.

"Not sure, I'm working here during the day, but I'll be free around six?"

"Tuesday's out, they're doing some sort of heater repair at the theater, so I have to do the work on Thursday."

We had a tradition by now. Henry had a mess of part time jobs, but my favorite was at the movie theater. It's a great little theater with only one screen but it plays a mix of new movies and old classics. Henry used to work there in the evenings during high school. Ushering with Medi, the both of them in their maroon vests and bow ties. The job wasn't self-sustaining for him after school, but by that time, it turned out he was the only one who knew how to rig up the projector. So on Tuesday nights these last twenty years, he goes by the theater once it's closed, and takes all the smaller reels splicing them together before feeding them onto one large disc. This disc goes into the projector creating the magic twists and turns, through gears and clips and is fed into a new giant disc. They go back and forth all weekend. Henry builds the movies over the course of the evening and then around midnight he plays the movie once to make sure everything's in the right order. He's the hero making it possible that we can traumatize our town youths with *The Exorcist* every fall. Well perhaps hero is a strong word, but I'm sure glad we have the movie theater. Anyway, he and I watch them together on their nightly playthrough. Nothing's more fun to me than a late night at the theater with Henry.

"Should be fine, probably better than fine to tell you the truth because this week, Friday is my day off."

"Great, it's a special movie," said Henry with his wonderful smile.

"Oh lovely," I replied sarcastically, "tell me."

I was anxious, because special in Henry's eyes could easily be a trap. Last week we watched a horror movie, which I could stand thanks to my sober state, but still it made me cringe just thinking about it. In truth, I watched my knee most of the evening.

"You'll just have to wait and see." He tossed a book high in the air, and I had to jump for it. Even through the haze of the massive crush, I shook my head disapprovingly but he wasn't there to see it. He was gone. I sighed a happy sound and smiled unrestrained before heading up towards the front desk and my last few hours of work.

5

ALL THERE IS

As soon as I sat down my cell phone started to ring. Well not really ring, but vibrate. It would be hard to pass out dirty looks at all the loud phones in the library if mine was ringing too. I slipped it out of my pocket and saw it was my mom. My mother dear, never has any boundaries when it comes to calling me at work. Generally, she's asking if I can grab something at the grocery on the way home, or wants to know where I saw the remote control last, or what channel *Jeopardy* is on. It's completely natural for me to silence her calls, several times while I'm at the desk. This was no exception, and so I finally just turned off the phone. I was still deep in daydreams about Henry.

I've got to say, I love Henry. That's pretty much all there is to it. It might be a bit weird, because Henry was my sister's boyfriend for years. He and Medi were together all through high school. All the proms and homecomings, they went to nearly each and every one of them. He's our neighbor and lives across the street from my parents.

Folks used to warn Medi and Henry about after high school. They said they probably wouldn't make it, that they were two very different people with different directions, but they just shrugged those worries off. The two of them stuck it out the first couple years that Medi went to college. Who knows how much of that, they were actually together for. It's hard for me to really know, since I was about nine when they broke up. I think it had to do with the fact that Henry was happy here. I've come to believe that there are two types of people in the world, people happy where they start and people who aren't happy until they leave.

The second group breaks into two more, those who stay gone and those who eventually come home.

Henry never was the leaving type. He was happy graduating and staying. Working at the movie theater, or the baseball field, or the zoo. Medi wanted more, always more, first it was college and then it was Milo. She met him there. He was becoming a doctor and maybe a doctor seemed better than an usher. Medi is actually two years older than Henry, and Milo is a couple years older than her. I remember she blamed Henry's age for a while as the reason they separated.

It was around the same time that they broke up that Henry's mom died. His father had never really been around, but his mother died tragically and I remember how sad the neighborhood felt. It was a really weird moment for young me, because of the breakup. It was like I needed to choose between Medi and Henry; and when Mrs. Hayden died it all turned on its head. Just seeing him alone at the house across the way. That's when it started, me ten years old, and him twenty. A childhood crush deep in the making. I remember going out of my way to see him. I would count the secret hellos in a notebook. Yes, it's super creepy, I know. I started to say hi to his mom in the cemetery too. It was just something to do. The cemetery was practically our backyard and it was easier to say hi, then to say nothing at all. It's a little weird for sure but she was our neighbor first and then she only moved to a plot about five hundred feet away.

Henry and I didn't grow a real friendship until years later. When it all started I was about 22 and he was around 32, and maybe, well not maybe, definitely I had drank a little too much this one night. I don't remember the evening too well. All I know is, I was at the local bar. There were a bunch of us. It must have been a weekend for a special football game or something, because lots of people were around. The bar was full and loud with music playing on the jukebox and the television was playing an old movie from my childhood, *The Princess Bride*. It was raining outside and everyone was spilling into each other's booths and standing hip to hip at the bar. I was with a bunch of girls I graduated high school with. Some of them I actually liked, and some of them it was more difficult to just not be friends with. One of the girls, Melanie St. Clair, was trying to get Henry's attention. He's gorgeous and if unlike me you didn't just fall near to pieces when he winks at you, it's a valid move to make. I couldn't fault her for that. This girl was really trying to work him, touching him, holding on to him, and I remember he just kept trying to ignore her. Finally, she got the hint he wasn't interested, but instead of walking away, she started shouting at him. She was saying some really nasty stuff and then she called him a moron, and that's when I lost it.

Henry was quiet. He never really liked school and I knew it wasn't some walk in the park. He and Medi would spend hours heads bent over books with notecards. I'd seen him with a giant line in his forehead, his finger following the words, his mouth moving slowly. He tried, and generally always succeeded, but school just wasn't easy for him. He might not have been a merit scholar but he was a friend and calling him a moron was a cheap asshole move and so without hesitation I punched this girl in the face. Let's face it, I probably wouldn't have hit her if I had been sober, but that's no excuse. It just happened, and to make it even worse or maybe better. I glanced at the television just at that moment and it was this scene in *The Princess Bride* where there is a dream sequence and this old lady starts booing Princess Buttercup because she gave up on true love. It was too loud to hear the TV. but the captions were there, and I read the words and half laughing I repeated it, "Boooooooooooooooo!" I shouted, "Booooooooo!"

I think we were all slightly shocked. Mel St. Jerk certainly was. She freaked out and tried to fight back. I would have done the same thing, I mean I punched her in her face, and pretty hard, but lucky for me as soon as she got to her feet she started to get sick. All the booze and the blow didn't seem to mix well. The bar staff was all over us. The front door was closest and they forced her out onto the sidewalk. She was surrounded by a crowd. I guess trying to avoid more violence I was escorted matter of factly out back and half shoved into a stinking damp alley.

I was really hyped up from all of it. I was nervous, I had never been in a fight with someone who didn't share my last name. I headed down the alley. It was only spitting rain by then, cold and miserable and my mind was there too. Part of me was afraid maybe this girl would find some sort of gang to help jump me. It was all intense, over blown scenarios on that walk home. I tried to get lost and made a short walk drag out but was more glad than ever when I saw our white two-story at the end of the street and there wasn't a pitchfork or police car insight. I was almost there, when I saw someone sitting on the front steps and to my real surprise it was Henry.

He stood up and I remember freezing, just watching him there. Me, not sure what to say, and wondering if he was going to say anything himself, then finally, he broke the silence. "I just wanted to make sure you got home alright."

"I'm alright," I nodded and went to step past him. I remember reaching out slightly to touch his arm, that was all, but the next minute I was leaning up, he was leaning down, and he was kissing me. It was really just one kiss, one long wonderful kiss.

After a moment he pulled back, and I heard him say, "Thanks, hey."

At least that's what it sounded like. I realized I wasn't the only one a bit drunk since *thanks hey* sounded more like *ooh save, to blave* or just some slightly affectionate jumble of words.

He was gone. That was the only time we've ever come close to being more than friends. Sure I've thought about it a lot. A definite lot, but that night was never mentioned again. I came and went over the next few years with school. Whenever I was home we would talk like we do. A couple times I went to the theater after he finished working on the reels to watch the movies, but it didn't become a regular thing until I moved home last year.

We started meeting up on Tuesday nights. I bring a six pack, of which I drink two and he drinks four. We sit in separate rows and shout stuff at each other. I climb up on the stage during the credits and dance in front of the lights, while he shouts out comments towards the production assistant and Best Boys, cheering the wonderful hospitality of Atlanta, and the approval of the ASPCA, and when we walk home after the movie, there are no light touches or wanting whispers, just laughs and smiles and friendly goodbyes. It's the best part of my week, and inside I know I love him, but the coward who takes up residence in my head and keeps one hand on my heart is too afraid to say anything. The truth is I enjoy going to the movies with him so much that I'm afraid to ruin that.

Even so, spending a few minutes with him is like a drug and it was going to help me make it through these next two hours. My mother couldn't invade my happiness, thoughts about Abe and Dad were shoved way back. It was only when Milo and Bennie arrived that I came back to reality.

6

DETERMINATION

I lifted my hand to wave with a smile and Milo nodded. He leaned over and whispered something to Bennie. I saw him kiss my nearly adult nephew on the forehead and then he left him there and walked across the room making a b-line for me. Milo is a good dad. He's got a fatherly way to him, and when he checks in on me, it's never annoying like when Medi does it. It just felt more natural, and probably it was just easier because I haven't seen as many childhood baby pictures of him in diapers like I had with Medi. He was kind and loving with his son, and so the kiss wasn't entirely out of character for him, but it felt odd in the moment. It shook me along with his blank and determined face. He didn't look happy to be there and seeing me.

"What brings you two here?" I said with a false customer service smile that I usually don't need with Milo, but I was wondering with more worry than I expected. Milo's face showed pain.

"Hon, can you leave early? Your mom sent me. We need you to come home."

"What's wrong?" I started to ask, but lifted my hand to cut off any response. I didn't want him to say whatever it was, not here at the library circulation desk. "I've got to run to the back. Can you give me a minute?"

"Of course," said Milo. "I'll be right up front with Ben."

Standing up, I didn't even glance at Carl who was sitting next to me. I'm sure he was doing his level best to appear not to be listening.

I crossed through the library easily enough. It was pretty empty, with just a few people probably working on homework, locked away in cubicles, trying to focus. It was a lucky night for me because my boss was there. Some Sundays, most Sundays, she's gone by then. Then it's just me and Carl closing, and leaving on those nights would've felt nearly impossible. I crossed from the hallway between the adult and kid's side of the library and passed into the staff only rooms. Turning into, my boss, Gayle's office, I found it empty and I was momentarily struck dumb.

Leading up to that moment I had been moving with smooth determination as if sleepwalking. Who knows what I would have said to her, but I was flowing and it would have gone from the walk to the words and hopefully nothing would have slowed me down, but here facing an empty office I was just frozen in my tracks, my mind went blank as my brain reset.

Shifting foot to foot I started wondering how much time I was letting pass. How long could I allow myself just to stand there. Though it felt like twenty minutes I knew it was probably sixty seconds at most. Finally, the door to the staff restroom opened and Gayle came out shaking her wet hands with a big smile, but something in my face seemed to poison her joy and her eyes shifted quizzically on mine.

"Hey, Gayle," I said, almost stuttering, no longer able to make eye contact, "I'm sorry but I've got to go home early. I'm not exactly sure why to tell you the truth, but my brother-in-law's out there. I think we're having a family emergency of sorts." I paused wondering if I had said enough, or said too much. I just kept going. "Actually I don't know," I laughed dryly, "I should have asked him for more information, but I just . . . I just . . . I . . . I've got to go, okay?"

"Sure," answered Gayle simply.

Of course, this was what she was going to say. This type of thing happened all the time in people's lives. Whatever this type of thing actually was? Luckily, it was a dead night with extra coworkers around.

I felt like I was stuck in something and my mind was stuttering as bad as my mouth. It was like those horror movie high feelings, equally natural and unnatural where every part of it was wrong. All bad feelings coming together to join forces. I turned around and looked for my bag, but after checking both the corner where I sometimes shove it and my locker, I remembered I had left the house abruptly that afternoon, leaving it behind.

I felt Gayle watching me and I turned without another word. I walked between the aisles of books and with one hand, I pushed a whole section of fiction back the way I hated. Not in line, not straight and tidy at all. My breath caught, then with hardly a glance to the circ desk I lifted my hand to Carl. He didn't seem confused which was a sure sign of his earlier listening ears.

Milo opened the door and led Bennie and I out into the parking lot. I grabbed onto Ben's arm. The action was more to steady myself than to help him to the car. I'm not sure if he recognized it. He leaned into me as much as I leaned into him. Sixteen, I realized. He was still just a kid, but also that little boy I'd always known was half grown. He's tall like his parents. It didn't take long until he passed me by and crowned me the shortest member of the family.

I couldn't ask questions or bring myself to speak. Instead, I stole a glance at my nephew trying to tell what sort of emotion he was feeling, but I wouldn't let myself make any predictions either. Disproving my fears with words or actions wasn't worth it, because my biggest fear was proving them right.

It was a quick drive, just minutes and when we pulled up to the house nothing looked wrong or out of sorts. There were lights on and cars that belonged, nothing extra. Just seeing it like that, for a moment I thought maybe I was worrying for nothing. It was probably some sort of dumb intervention over what I had said to Dad earlier. I remembered when I was ten, and during a fight, running out of things to say and so I shouted, "You're not even my dad." That was the worst thing I had ever said to him and it hadn't made him sad, it made him angry. Anger that he took out on my ass. I shook my head relieved, almost looking forward to the shouting that I hoped to find. I took a deep breath and tried to smile. That was it, I was sure of it. Or maybe something even more dumb, like Mom was calling me home because it was defcon infinity to find her favorite coffee mug that I sometimes used. Maybe, hopefully, I was freaking out over nothing. This thought brought me too far afield and into the ridiculous, and so I was back to worried again, but I clung to that hope and for a second I was almost relaxed. I opened the door and climbed out to wait on the others, but inside the car Bennie and Milo started talking, not following me and I felt extremely separated from them at that moment. Separate from the house, separate from the car. I needed to figure this out and I knew I had to push onward, and so with more determination I headed up the path, gripped the doorknob and stepped inside.

The house was as it always was. I froze and listened. I searched for the drone of the little kitchen television set, but I couldn't hear it. A sound on the steps caught my attention, and I looked up to see Mom coming down to the landing. She looked different somehow. She might have been the same tall, thin, classy, lady with quizzical eyes and beauty shop curls, but this woman wasn't the mother I'd seen yesterday. She was changed. She looked alone. It might sound dumb, or impossible to describe, but she looked like, well like a widow. It was without a word or a glance that I knew all those unspoken fears were true. My father was dead.

There was a chair next to the door and I felt my knees buckling beneath me. I sat down and looked at my hands; they folded open and closed into fists, moving like breaths, or waking flower petals.

Mom cut the space between us and crouched down in front of me, and touched my knees before taking my hands in hers.

"Emlyn," she said calmly, "Dad's gone."

I couldn't look at her and she pushed on.

"What is it you kids used to say? He's finally tall enough to ride the roller coaster."

I coughed a disbelieving laugh. I couldn't believe that she remembered that terrible joke that we hung on to as children. *Heaven's Gate*, that cult name that we inappropriately turned into a roller coaster straight to heaven. A mighty loopty loop through the clouds, or that sudden psych where your stomach falls and it drops to the big fires. It was such a dumb joke that we made whenever we stole a spot in the back garden, and replaced the marigolds with hamsters or goldfish.

She stopped talking, and waited on me to say something, but I just wouldn't take the bait. I couldn't. It didn't make sense, and I shook my head, before finding my voice.

"I don't understand? What happened? I saw him this afternoon, eating tomato soup, sitting at the kitchen table." Pulling one hand free, I gestured almost violently doubting the things I heard.

"What happened?" I repeated with rising volume.

I was angry at him for acting so normal that afternoon. But truthfully, I knew what happened, I happened. I remembered more than soup, I remembered our argument and the things I had said. He had told me he was sick and I had shook him off and called him a liar. I had walked out on him. In that moment of remembering, I thought I might puke.

"He'd been sick for a while. For weeks he'd been looking for the right time to tell you kids, but he said he couldn't bring himself to do it. We thought maybe when everyone was up next month for Thanksgiving. What a great holiday that would have been." Mom laughed a painful sound and her hand that was holding on to me shook.

"But, he seemed fine."

"He was your dad, of course he seemed fine. The thing about you kids is you only ever see what you want to see. Your parents don't change, and sorry to tell you, but you don't change either. When I see Abraham, I still see that boy with all the curls and the tricycle." She shrugged as an explanation.

"It was Dad's heart," came a voice from the kitchen doorway. Medi had snuck in. Her eyes were red from crying. She's a crier, but I couldn't blame her. She crossed the room and pulled both Mom and I into a hug. We were locked in, trapped in this family tragedy. A family tragedy that I knew was of my making.

7

COMING UNDONE

I wanted to get away. It wasn't a good hug. It wasn't a joyful hug. It was a bear trap I was locked up in with my sister sobbing next to my ear. Thankfully the door opened and Milo appeared, so Medi shifted her grasp from us allowing Mom and I to break free. Mom stayed close with her hand on Medi's back. This was much more natural for her. She's not much of a hugger. Dad was the hugger, just thinking of that my stomach dropped. I pulled deeper into the house, away from the emotion of the entryway. My path took me into the kitchen, with its silent television and kitchen table covered in many neat piles. Seeing it like that, like it should be but with that one missing piece, was too much. I glanced toward the sink and the dish rack and saw the bowl and the pot that the soup had been made in. Dad must have washed them after I left.

I realized, I didn't know what had happened. Where had he died? When had he died? It had only been hours, not even five hours. Mom had called my phone not long ago, was he alive then? I wanted to scream. I set my hand against my forehead and realized I was close to coming completely undone.

Stepping closer to the backdoor was the recycling bin and there on top was the tomato soup can, it had been washed clean for the trash. I picked it up and with a complete feeling of running for my life went out the back door. I crossed through the side yard. It was dark out, but lights from the house made squares of yellow against the tall fence. It felt like a prison spotlight I needed to avoid.

I knew where I was going. It was the place I always ran away to while growing up. Across the cemetery and up the hill where the old playground sat. I was too big for the slide and most of the equipment, but I would still sit on the rubber swings with their heavy chains and pump my legs, trying to shake off whatever was bothering me at the time. All my life it had been the same.

The cemetery closed at dark so theoretically the playground was closed as well, but there were no gates that locked us out and the neighborhood watched over it. It wasn't until I was halfway up the road that I heard the laughter and saw the shapes of several teenage kids, doing what we had done in our past lives. Small town rulebreakers. I hadn't started crying yet. My hand grasped the metal soup can, I could just feel the give and held on just strong enough to manipulate the shape without actually bending it. Seeing the kids I was bubbling with anger. They were at my spot and I needed it more than them. I was rooted in place, not knowing where to go, and so I walked where my legs led and ended up by Henry's mom's grave. I fell into a heap still gripping the can and burying my face in the crook in my elbow, I started to cry.

"Oh Dad, oh Dad, what have I done? Oh Dad, I'm so sorry. Wake up, wake up, wake up," I cried, repeated and pleaded, rocking myself, closing my eyes and hoping it was all a bad dream. I couldn't control it. There was such a wave of emotion like I had never felt before in happiness or sadness, not even terror. A noise came out of me, a keening that turned to a sob and I realized anyone in the near vicinity would have heard it and believed I was a ghost with off tune wailing. I buried my head into the collar of my shirt and just cried, rocking myself naturally and feeling like I was the last person on earth, strangely wanting to be the last person on earth. Nothing mattered. My dad was dead and there was a good chance I had something to do with it.

Eventually, I settled myself down somehow. There were a couple napkins from lunch in my pocket and I was able to blow the gallon of snot free from my head. Wiping my eyes on my shirt, I laid back across the grave. I needed time. I don't know why it became so important to

me that when I went back home I would look normal, free of this emotion. For some reason I needed it. My head ached, and I took a breath,
breathing out and watching the small chilly cloud rise up and disappear
from sight. The stars were out that night. It was a nice cold evening.
Brisk, that's a word my dad would use. *Put on your hat, it's brisk out.* I
smiled painfully.

Sitting back up looking around the cemetery. I noticed that way off,
the playground stood empty. I wondered if the kids had heard me and
realized the place wasn't so cool or fun anymore. I contemplated going
up there, but not much. Holding the soup can, I ran my thumb across
the wrinkly wrapper feeling the can's grooves beneath. The paper must
have gotten wet when my father held it under the faucet to clean it. I
lifted it to my nose and the smell of tomato was long gone, but the soapy
clean scent seemed to still be there, lingering.

I let my right hand run through the grass beneath me. It was harsh
grass, fall grass ready to be treated poorly by the winter. I wondered how
happy the groundskeepers would be to not have to mow any longer. I
never felt guilty sitting here on Mrs. Hayden's grave. Caroline the stone
said. She was never a Caroline to me living, I doubted she would ever be
in death; Mrs. Hayden. I tried to think about her, remember her. She
had this short brown hair, it was a light color like a field mouse. She had
glasses and had a sweet motherly way about her. She wore sweatshirts
with cats and wildflowers. She had blue eyes that she'd given to her son.
It must have been so hard for Henry to lose her. To feel alone. It helped
a bit to remember how lucky I was. I was far from alone.

"Oh, Dad," I muttered under my breath and felt my eyes starting to
leak again. I wiped them roughly, and growled, swallowing all the extra
liquid that seemed to be caught up in my throat and nose.

"Mrs. H," I started and was glad to hear my voice sounded almost
normal, "show him around, okay? Tell him, yeah, tell him, well, you
know, tell him that I love him."

I had enough of it then and with my pockets full of damp napkins
and my hand still gripping the soup can I headed home, walking down

the hill through the stones, watching my steps in the shadows of the old oak trees with roots that seemed to live to upend civil war era graves.

The cemetery butts up against Henry's house and backyard. It was a ghostly arrangement and we spent a lot of our childhoods, me and Llew, and before us Medi, Henry and Abe sneaking out of the house and running between the headstones; daring each other and trying to scare ourselves stupid. Llew was the one who ended up ruining it all when he tripped over a small marker and twisted his ankle so badly a neighbor called the police thinking there were black magic sacrifices going on.

I stepped over the short stone fence that separates the cemetery from the dead end and was caught off guard, because not too far away Medi and Henry were talking. Henry had his arms around her and she had her head firmly planted in his chest. It was the sort of thing that was normal twenty plus years ago, but seemed strange now, until I remembered my sister's father just died.

Henry looked up and saw me. He whispered something to my sister and the two of them came apart. He waved slightly, as if he wasn't sure a wave was the right response for someone whose father had just died. Medi's face was the type of face I was worried mine would look like ten minutes ago when I was trying to clean it up. That ugly crying face we all pray not to have when watching the simple perfect tears shed by people in movies. She tried to wave me over, but again face planted into Henry.

Part of me thought I should be there for my sister, and save Henry from her extreme grief, but I couldn't be with them. I just couldn't. I didn't want to share my loss. I moved as quickly as I could beside the house and around to the back door. Inside the kitchen I saw my mother standing in front of the brewing coffee pot and talking steadily and calmingly through the phone. She smiled sadly at me when she heard the door close, but soon turned back and away. Feeling lucky that she was the same woman I had left and who I expected to find, I left the room and went upstairs to my bedroom.

The room seemed untouched by sadness. With the door closed I could hear no sounds from the rest of the house, thick walls and heavy wood seemed to do a lot to keep others away at that moment. The room was clean, I had just cleaned it that weekend, before heading off to spend the night with Brynn. I'd gotten so used to moving these last few years. Not to say I wasn't a packrat; we were a family of near hoarders. My father was the neat one, and he dealt with our mess with piles. A trait I in turn had adopted. Everywhere and out of sight were piles. Under the bed, in the closet. I could see a new pile on top of the chair. It looked like laundry and mail.

I don't know how many times I had tried to tell my parents I did my own laundry, but they snuck around the room, as if waiting for a sock to be laid down just to have the excuse to do a load. I couldn't bring myself to look at the basket, to see who the culprit was this time. The socks, it was always in the socks. My mother was a sock baller, my father a folder.

As quickly as I could, I crossed the room and flipped off the light. Stumbling about, I reached in my bag and pulled out the headphones and put them on. Without another word I kicked off my shoes and climbed fully clothed under the covers. I forced myself to try and sleep. I drowned in the smooth piano music that was usually so peaceful and now seemed to be played note by note against my skull, but eventually something clicked off and I slept.

8

MONDAY, BUT NOT YET MONDAY

I woke up in perfect clarity knowing my father was dead. It was the last thought I went to sleep with and it was something I knew as a fact when I first opened my eyes. The room was quiet and unchanged, and I was completely awake. The red lights of the alarm clock showed it was half past two. I couldn't remember what time it was when I had gone to sleep, and I walked back through the night before. Milo had come to get me and I had left work early, how long I stayed awake in the cemetery, in my wanderings were without true definition, but it couldn't have been long. Sitting up I felt uncomfortable. I was almost fully dressed, locked up in layers with stiff jeans and a bra. My heavy brick of a phone was in my pocket; I pulled it free. Turning it back on, I saw it was full of text messages piled one on top of the other. I didn't care to read them and instead tossed the phone across the room letting it land on my backpack before sliding with a thump to the hardwood floor. I saw the soup can sitting on my desk and a chill ran up my spine.

A cigarette, that's what I wanted. One of my first thoughts was the realization that Dad wouldn't be able to catch me this time. He hated my smoking, hated it more than most anything, probably because we all seemed to go through phases of it. From one sibling to the next we smoked for several years and then eventually seemed to grow out of it. It made no sense, but maybe the smoking was as genetic as the ability to stop. I kept waiting to stop, to really want to give it up. It seemed like maybe this was the moment, something to dedicate to my father, but I knew today wasn't a day to quit.

Through the house, all was quiet. The lights were on, and I found myself flipping them off, creating a path of darkness from the hallway to the stairway, through the foyer and into the kitchen. I went out the screen door and lowered myself onto the back steps. The cigarette felt great once it was lit. Something about it, just smoking, doing something so simple in such a quiet moment gave me something to focus on and something to consider far from everything else.

"Fuck," I whispered, feeling a wave of cold and pushing my hands up into my sleeves, stealing my body's warmth. There was nothing much more to say, just a feeling that needed to come out to the quiet night. Yet I wasn't so alone after all.

"Caught," came a voice behind me, and though it should have scared the shit out of me, I didn't react for a long moment. The energy and ability to be frightened was missing. I glanced back knowing the voice.

"Hey Mom."

She opened up the screen door and sat down next to me. "You got one of those for me, kid?"

This I reacted to, having just spent so much time thinking about how alone I was in this bad habit. Handing her a cigarette. I watched her light it. It was the strangest thing seeing her perform the act.

"Don't tell your father," she said and then shuttered. I couldn't tell if it was a real statement or a joke.

She reached out and took my hand.

We sat in silence for a few moments before I said, "I didn't know you smoked?"

"I don't," she said and winked at me. "Oh kid, I don't know how we're going to make it through these next few days."

"I'm sorry I wandered off earlier," I said, feeling guilty.

"That's why I have four kids, one of you is always in striking distance. I'm sure you'll get your chance to be needed. Your brothers should be here in the afternoon. Amos, Brynn and Fletcher the day after. We'll have a full house. I think Medi is pretty well dug in as well."

"Are Bennie and Milo here?" I asked. They lived close enough that they could leave and come back pretty easily.

"Mm-hmm," she nodded.

"Maybe, I'll go stay at the bookstore," I said half-laughing.

"Don't do that," said Mom in all seriousness. She let go of my hand and got up, picking up a piece of cardboard that seemed to have blown loose from the outside recycling.

"I was just joking," I said defensively.

"No you weren't Emlyn," she answered sternly enough that she had my attention. "You need to be here for this. You have a way of disappearing. I know you don't like these moments. No one does, but you can't just pretend it didn't happen. You do and you'll regret it. I need you here young lady. Your family needs you, and whether you admit it or not, you need us."

The *young lady* made me glance away from her face and back to my hand and the cigarette and it's growing ash. It was difficult to hear that earnest disappointment. I shook my head.

"Mom," I said, swallowing hard and choking on my worries, "I should tell you, Dad and I, we had a fight this morning."

She waved her hands as if shooing away smoke, or just shutting me down before I said anything more. "Your father loved you, and you loved him. Whatever you argued over, it doesn't matter."

I nodded.

"Look at me," she said just as firmly. "There's nothing you could have said that would have changed the way he felt."

I nodded again.

"You know that right?"

"Sure, of course. It's just." I shook my head.

"Yeah," Mom agreed, "it's always just." She smiled, reaching out to push the loose hair away from my eyes and then walked back into the house.

I finished the cigarette and realized it was too cold to be sitting here. My skin prickled up and my breath looked like smoke far removed from my transgressions. Rubbing my arms again, I knew it was time to go back inside, but I didn't want to. I felt hidden here, distant. My mother was right, I liked to hide, to be alone in my sadness, in all of it. I doubted that would change. I wasn't going to become Medi, loud and open in my emotions, unafraid to show how I felt, but nor could I turn them off. This wasn't going anywhere.

I got up, moving slowly and went back into the house. My mother had disappeared somewhere. She could move silently, she was that poem about fog and little cat feet. Wherever I stepped, I heard the house creaking all around me. Back up to my room, I ducked in the bathroom and brushed my teeth, then I shivered. I pulled off my clothes and changed into sleep pants, taking off my bra and socks. The cold seemed to have come with me and it was easy to crash back into the bed and climb under the covers. It was still fall and freezing temperatures hadn't set in just yet, but they were knocking. In the coming months I might see my breath inside my room as well, my father counting every penny was a stern believer that we all just needed to dress more appropriately; the thermostat under his watchful gaze. Those days were still far off, for now the cold weather helped create the most comfortable sleeping environment, and as much as my emotions didn't want to rest I was able to ignore them for the moment and knew more sleep would be there for the taking, and so I took it.

9

BROTHERS

"Lyn," my sister said loudly from the doorway. "Hey, Lynman," she repeated.

"Yeah," I grumbled, pulling the pillow off my head, where it seemed to have settled.

"We're going to go pick up Llew from the airport, do you want to come?"

"No," I said flatly, and turned over. I would see him soon enough.

"Suit yourself," she said with some disappointment in her voice. "We'll be back in a couple hours, unless we stop for lunch. Are you sure?"

I didn't think about it much. I knew I should join them, but I just couldn't seem to muster the energy for it all. Llew was much more like Medi in the fact that they both talked at volumes that shared conversations with strangers, and I was sure it would be a very tear filled reunion that I would happily skip.

"I'll be here when you all get back."

"Okay, well, help clean things up, why don't you? We'll be sure to have visitors."

"Yup," I muttered, before burying my head back under the pillow. The door closed and I faded back into the comfortable territory that could trap me between sleep and waking.

It was hours later when I finally climbed out of bed. I opened the door slightly and heard nothing, only silence. I figured they had all gone to get Llew. They would be home soon and I didn't feel guilty about not cleaning up. I knew it was just Medi trying to give me a chore since I didn't choose the family's company. I caught myself mentally bitching about Medi and I realized I was being mean. I took a breath and sighed. This was going to be hard on all of us and if she needed me to spend a few minutes outside of my comfort zone I was sure I could do that. It was the least I could do when I killed her father. I shook my head, but didn't tell myself I was wrong.

First thing I did was pick up my phone, ignoring all of the text messages, and scrolled to my boss's number. As much as I wanted to text her, I couldn't bring myself to be that person, and so I hit the call number. To my great happiness it was her voicemail I ended up speaking with and in as few words as possible I explained that my father had died, and I would need to take some days off. Probably the whole week. Hopefully that would work and to let me know if there were any issues with that request. It all felt so business like and dumb, but I was glad that I could treat it that way. Tossing the phone back down I hopped into the shower, and quickly cleaned up and got dressed into comfy clothes. The old jeans where the cuffs had been trampled into threads, and the t-shirt with the holes and shiny armpits that I guessed was brought on from the deodorant and its chemical ingredients. I hid under my maroon hooded zip-up, with sleeves that had been set on fire by cigarettes and drunk hands too many times. It was a set of clothes not long from the trash bin, but it was comfortable, fuck it.

The same tired hazel eyes and dusty brown hair looked back from the mirror. I had a hard time catching my own glance. Dressed, I wandered out of my room, listening to the house around me, curious if everyone went with Medi to pick up Llew or not. It sure seemed like it. Doors stood open and silent, the light came through the windows making everything seem comfortable and inviting. That autumn sun, without all the harshness of the summer months made it easy to find a chair and just sit. *Fall is for reflection*, Dad used to say.

I thought I might pick around the kitchen, I wasn't hungry which seemed strange since I only had the grilled cheese on the way to work yesterday. Maybe I was hungry, but my insides still just felt so twisted it was hard to tell the difference between the tight ball of anxiety or the tight ball that was my stomach. Pushing through the kitchen door, I was stopped in my tracks by the surprise that I wasn't alone after all. There was someone else with the same idea, bent over staring into the fridge and pushing through Tupperware. He glanced back when he heard the creak of the door.

Abraham, the mystery that is my brother, who I had just realized gave me half of my DNA, stood up to meet me. I hadn't expected him yet. I figured he would drive to get here, but he must have left in the middle of the night to have arrived so soon. He was well dressed, neat, and generally the exact opposite of me. Tall and thin with short wavy hair that's started to lighten and just the beginning of a shadow on his cheeks. Abe has a stern look, but always with a smile that softens his edges. Without a word he left the refrigerator door wide open and walked over to hug me.

"Hey Abe," I said, surprised to hear my voice break.

"Hey kiddo," he said in response. Our conversation was lost, muttered in shoulders and hair. It was a long hug, more than that it was the type of hug Dad would always give, not half assed but whole assed, completely engaged. We would always laugh, but relish them. He never stopped hugging first. I wanted to cry and I wanted to never let go of Abe, but somehow we both came apart. His eyes were wet and I turned away just long enough to wipe my own.

"You must not have gotten any sleep last night, I mean to be here already."

"Yeah, it seemed to make the most sense to do something with the time. I was keeping Fletcher up, tossing and turning. He wouldn't say anything, but it seemed wrong to keep both of us from sleeping."

"He'll be here tomorrow?" I asked.

"Probably Wednesday morning," said Abe and glanced back at the refrigerator. "Work keeps him busy."

"I would think he's about old enough to retire," I ribbed him. We always made fun of Fletcher because he was a good eight years older than Abe, and when the two of them first met it certainly felt like a bigger gap then it did now.

"So, where is everyone?" he asked. "It was spooky showing up, I thought the house was empty. I thought you were a ghost."

"They caravanned off to pick up brother dear. I don't think anyone expected you until later. Are you hungry?" I said, curious why he kept looking at the fridge.

"No, but I keep thinking I should eat. I kept waiting for Dad to ask if I was planning to cool off the whole house."

"Our fiscally responsible father," I said. Dad used that phrase a lot, fiscally responsible. He wanted us all to be fiscally responsible. "Our father," I repeated at a whisper to myself, but loud enough that Abe heard me. I was curious about what was going on in my brother's brain. If he ever thought of me as more than his sister.

"Eggs," he finally said.

"What?" I asked, thinking I had missed part of the conversation.

"I'm going to make eggs, you're going to make coffee." He squeezed my shoulder when he said it.

"That I can do," I said, and was glad to have something to keep me busy for a few minutes. Spooning heaping after heaping spoonfuls of the amazing smelling grounds into the machine. I thought about the fact that we were all trained to drink coffee black. Growing up that was the only way it was made in our house. It kept us from drinking it when we were young. I noticed my father sometimes sneaking a bit of milk in the side, but my mother felt drinking black coffee was one of the most important skills to teach us. Usually when she spoke about it the words turned into a lecture on self-reliance.

Abe came close and reached above me to the top cabinet that was out of my grasp. I was confused for a minute about what he was hoping to find. I thought maybe he was looking for the paper towels, though I should have known better. You live somewhere all your life and there are things you never forget, like where the phone books are kept, the Poison Control sticker on the door frame, and the junk drawer full of old batteries and hair ties. Abe reached high and took the bottle of whiskey that was always there. I never saw it get replaced, but its levels seemed to change every once and awhile to show it wasn't forgotten.

"Make mine Irish while you're at it," he said and smiled.

"That sounds like the best idea I've heard in a while." I poured large coffees with large shots, and we both flinched at the taste, but it didn't stop either of us from taking a second sip directly. He plated up the eggs, while I went ahead and buttered a couple pieces of toast. Neither of us spoke during this time. I loved Abe because of it. He and I were both like this, we got it from Mom. This quiet calm, with hours of silence that is comfortable and inviting. Dad, Medi and Llew are the chatty ones, who don't seem to be able to deal with silence in their surroundings or each other. There would be TV on, music on, the radio on, talking, words climbing on top of each other, shouting questions from the other room. When it was just Mom, Dad and I. Mom and I spent a lot of time exchanging looks, while Dad narrated to fill in the space. Just the thought, the guilt of making fun of him and the knowledge that days would be quieter made me lay down the butter knife.

Abe seemed to notice. "You alright?" he asked even though we both knew there was no way we were alright.

"Yeah, sure, I mean no. He's missing. I'm not ready for him to be missing. I'm not ready to even miss him, I saw him yesterday, but he's fucking missing."

My brother swallowed hard and looked everywhere. He looked all around the kitchen and his eyes were starting to get wet again, and I felt bad for turning what was maybe a nice breakfast into these feelings. Yet, if he was going to say anything, or if he was going to cry. He didn't get the chance, because the minute he seemed determined to push on, the backdoor flew open and the rest of our family appeared.

The people known for their loudness shouted, and Abe with his wet eyes started to laugh to see how happy they were to see him. Llew was the first person to hug him, the two of them tall men. Llew kissed him on the mouth, and then shook him senseless. Llew outgrew all of us, and though I'm sure Abe could have held his own if it ever came to that, we all just let Llew manhandle us as was his way.

The two of them were soon swarmed by my mom and Medi into one giant hug, which I was happy to watch, but it wasn't over before Medi seemed to notice I was missing and shouted, "Newman family hug, get over here Lyn." Soon several hands were grabbing my face and my shoulders and I was part of the monster.

"Alright," Abe said to my happiness. "Let me breathe, -oh god, Llew did you just lick my fucking ear?"

"I love you big brother, okay, Lynman, my Lynman, come here," he demanded and pushed Abe away as if he was a stranger on the street and took hold of me. He hugged me so tight I felt my shoulders shrink, and kissed my hair and my forehead. Finally, he tired out and wrapped his arms around me like he was a heavy scarf. Llew was a lot, and as different as the two of us are, he's still my best friend.

If a day doesn't go by without some sort of text, call or obnoxious photo I get to worry. He's not someone I can ignore, nor against all my best efforts is he someone I want to. He's about the closest I'll ever get to a twin, all this said, he annoys the shit out of me.

"Why didn't you meet me at the airport?"

"I didn't feel the need to cause a public scene," I said, breaking free of his grip and sliding around the table to sit down with my breakfast.

"Coffee, coffee, coffee," he said, grabbing my cup, taking a sip and half choking before coughing loudly. I glanced at Abe and we both laughed.

"Sorry if it's too strong," I said.

"You kids," said Mom and walked out of the room.

Llew passed the mug to Medi, who went to take a sip, but stopped when it got close to her face. "I hope this mug isn't planning on driving anywhere."

"So you want one?" asked Llew, taking the mug back, enjoying another sip and then passing it back over to me.

Medi gestured with her thumb and pointer, showing a smidge of space. "Just a taste."

Llew clapped and walked over to the coffee pot.

"You trust him to pour a little?" asked Abe.

Medi laughed but did walk over to supervise the pouring.

I started to eat my plate of eggs quickly, knowing once Llew was back he wouldn't think twice about taking the plate himself. I realized I was actually hungry once I started eating and wanted to protect my food better than I protected the coffee.

"Why didn't you want to cause a scene?" hollered Llew. "Our fucking father is dead, this is exactly the moment when you do cause a scene. It's our right." He came back over and sat down next to me. He claimed the second triangle of toast and used it to scoop up any overlooked crumbs on the plate.

"You're right, if I wanted to cause a scene this would be the perfect time for it, but since I don't ever like to be on center stage for the rental car set, I'm perfectly good watching said scene in our kitchen."

"Llew's right," Medi chimed in as I knew she would. "You hold back your emotions and it's not healthy."

"Nobody is holding back their emotions. These are my emotions. Sorry we run at different volumes."

Medi's eyebrows shot up and I knew she felt like I was picking on her. This was one of our go-to arguments. She always thought I was trying to quiet her down, because I was, but I could hardly feel bad for saying what I did. I really didn't feel like I needed her to tell me how to grieve.

"Sorry, what was that? Speak up," said Llew. "Mumble mumble mumble Lynman the mumbler. This is how we know you're adopted."

"Cheers," I said, ignoring him, just happy that he took her side so she wouldn't get defensive. I lifted my mug and my siblings followed suit.

"To Dad," toasted Abe. We clinked our old chipped mugs together and smiled sadly. The whiskey made me warm.

10

WANDER AND WONDER

Things took off around the house soon after we finished our coffee. The phone started ringing only to be interrupted by the doorbell. I tried to stay busy cleaning, washing dishes and sweeping the kitchen floor. Mom had an appointment with the funeral home and Llew went with her. Medi directed the flow of people and the cleaning. She would be straight-faced for a while but would fall into tears the next. The visitors who started to appear with pies or casseroles, only meant to stop for a minute, but curiosity pulled them into conversations. I learned the most about how Dad died from these chats.

He had felt weak in the afternoon and wanted to go to the hospital, though he thought he might take a nap and feel better first. Mom went to wake him up for dinner and found him acting strange. Together they went to the emergency room, and just minutes after getting there, he sat down in the waiting room and just died. His heart gave out. He was gone so quickly that they couldn't do anything even sitting inside a hospital.

The knowledge that he probably wouldn't have felt weak or ill if I had only kept my mouth shut that day haunted me. I could have listened to his worries about me leaving home. I could have told him I would think about it, but no instead I called him a liar and walked out on him. I felt sick just thinking about it. I was sure that it was all my fault.

After a while I needed to get out. I followed the familiar path to the backdoor. I wanted to smoke, but with so many people around I didn't want to be caught by a crowd. I thought maybe I would wander around the cemetery, but the minute I was out, I came face to face with Abe, who was trying to force a trash bag into a relatively full barrel.

"Remind me when trash day is?" he said with his hands on his hips.

"Tomorrow, I think. We should bring it out tonight."

He looked at me and smiled. "What are you up to?"

"Not much, just going on a wander."

"Why not wander over with me to Dad's store. Mom called. She needs me to get some paper's out of the safe."

"Sure," I said, happy to get away from the house for a minute.

"Let me go wash my hands," said Abe before heading back inside the house.

I sat down on the steps to wait for him. I heard the water running for a minute and the sound of the doorbell again. I leaned into the stone wall that ran beside the steps and watched a spider move along the groove of the stone. Hidden inside the crack was the spider's egg sack. She seemed to be checking on it before scurrying back out, running her little spider errands. I wondered about her day. Work on the web, check. Mummify a fly, check. Don't get washed down a spout, check.

It probably was a lot of work being a spider, a lot of responsibility. I was curious how many spiders would just shout fuck you to the job and go blow away on the wind like all those spider babies in *Charlotte's Web*.

Caught up in spiderland it took a few minutes before I realized that I'd been waiting a long time for Abe, and so I wandered back into the house. I found Milo and Bennie putting away groceries. They must have been tasked with all the extra food we would be eating. I reached up to fluff Bennie's hair and peered into the bag he was emptying. I winked at Milo.

"How are you two?" I asked, having not seen them since last night.

"Keeping busy," said Milo, "do you need anything Lynman?"

"Nah, I'm good. How about you two? Do you need anything?"

They both shook their heads. I sighed heavily and Bennie smiled, making me smile in return.

"You guys know who's upfront?"

"Sorry," Milo said, Bennie just shrugged.

I heard the sound of several voices speaking in the foyer, and crossed softly through the house, hoping to judge if it was a conversation I would mind getting pulled into. Peaking around the corner I saw Abe but I realized I couldn't see who he was chatting with and so I just bit the bullet and crossed out of hiding.

Standing in the door with his arms crossed was Henry. He had his guarded smile and I knew it was a happy conversation that he considered might be inappropriate in these mournful times. Shoot, I realized I knew him too well. He saw me come into the room and his tight grin stretched into something real. Abe saw me and reached out to grab my shoulder. Medi seemed joyful as well.

"I tell you," she said, "I wish Dad was here to see this. The three of us together. Abe, Henry and I. It's cute, isn't it Lynny, you must feel about eight years old again, seeing us standing here laughing." She grabbed onto Henry's arm and it was good to see her happy, even though my most natural emotion of annoyance with my sister was trying to flare up.

Not wanting to get too wrapped up in her reminisce; I smiled politely, before saying, "I'll see you out front when you're ready Abe."

"I'm ready," he answered. "Henry, I'll talk to you soon." They exchanged the strange half hugs that you see men do; part handshake, part back slap, a whole oddity.

I didn't look at Henry, as I squeezed by and out the door. I didn't know why I was ignoring him. Just yesterday, seeing Henry at the library lightened my day and gave me the joy and hope that I needed to turn a difficult situation bright. It was a curiosity I would continue to ignore. Abe and I left Henry and Medi, and walked down the steps, and headed up the road.

Town isn't so big. The main street is the old highway and though we miss a lot of traffic now that it has changed, we still get the old timers and folks looking for a pretty drive. Not too far off, you'll find the big grocery stores and even further on strip malls full of any and everything, but here we have those spots that make it feel like your whole world can exist in a few blocks. The post office with its red brick and gothic columns, the small grocery store where local kids fill their pockets with candy of all shapes and sizes before leaving the wrappers all across the movie theater's aisles. The bank, the library, a couple churches, a couple more pizza places, the antique shop and of course Dad's book store.

I've always been amazed that he can stay in business. He does well, or I guess did well. He supplied the college textbooks and required reading that younger student's need. He's got a small back room filled up with more than just books, but old video games and board games. Growing up our house was almost always in the process of putting together some old puzzle my dad had found somewhere or another, a garage sale or random bookstore donation. It was our job to check them before they went on the sale shelf. I've seen more pictures of Swiss castles or baskets of kittens than anyone my age has any right to have seen. I'm glad our town seems to cherish this place. I've seen people look at the books like they are some sort of a mystery, knowing a digital copy can be more easily found online or free from the library, but they'll shell out a couple bucks every week or so and chat with Dad over a cup of coffee.

It was so hard to imagine what would happen to the store now that Dad was gone. It didn't even make sense to think about it, and I pushed this worry aside. When we finally arrived out front, I leaned in the doorway watching Abe take it all in. Fiction's Family, it read in old chipped paint. It was an odd name. Out of towners came in and would ask for Mr. Fiction. We always just laughed, hardly able to explain, making up stories about our black sheep in-laws Nonfiction's Family, having constant sales over history books or biographies just so people knew we had it all. *We like all books here*, Dad would say. We complained about the occasional confusion, but never imagined changing the name.

I saw the store practically every day but it had been a while for Abe. After a minute I realized he would be waiting on me, because I was the one with the key. I dug them out glad they had been in my pocket and not hanging up at home. The door swung open and inviting and my hand almost flipped the closed sign over before letting it drop back down to an empty fist.

Everything was as it should be. Light came down through the windows and slatted blinds, illuminating rays in ladder-like slits across different shelves. Tiny dust ghosts traveling on sunbeams. I led Abe through the building and to the back office. It was a small room, with a desk and a computer, and a second chair wedged in for any visiting guests. Abraham dropped down in Dad's chair before looking at me with that sad smile.

"I think this chair and this office is one of the most constant things in my life. I'm thinking it's the same chair. Could that be possible? I mean he would have certainly gotten something better." Abe popped up snatching the piece of furniture along the way, grabbing the legs and holding it upside down like he was going to shake the pennies from its pockets. "Same chair," he said and pointed.

On one of the legs I saw a sloppy number sixteen. "Get it?" he said and slapped my shoulder hard.

"The sixteenth president not to be confused with our Abey Baby," I replied using my brother's old nickname with his lucky number borrowed from both his birthday and Mr. Lincoln's presidency. "What did you use, and why?"

"I think it was a nail file, and why? I don't know, kids are dumb. I was dumb." He shrugged.

"Youthful vandal, if only you were famous and then it would be worth something."

"I'll have Mom appraise it . . . priceless."

He set the chair right and sat back down before swiveling around to the safe wedged in the corner. "You know Fletcher and I have been talking about moving to town?"

"Really?" This was a true surprise. Abe and his husband were both lawyers in D.C., busy and involved with their lives there.

"Yeah, it would be nice to be closer to the city, close to mom and I sort of miss it here. Actually, I really miss it here. I was talking to Dad yesterday-"

"You and Dad spoke yesterday?" I said with a sharp edge that showed much more concern than I wanted, but actually it felt like someone had dumped a bucket of cold water on me.

He glanced away from the safe and back towards me. "Yeah, lucky, huh? I'm so glad I got the chance."

I realized he wasn't really paying attention to me when he said that and I was relieved, but still worried about how much of the conversation Dad and I shared was of wider knowledge.

"What did you two talk about?" I pried, hoping I sounded nonchalant in the asking.

"Different things, he mentioned you were thinking of going back to school. I think he was hoping I might be able to talk you out of it. I think he saw the two of us working here together. Surprised?"

"What?"

"You probably think you have the patent on life changing choices."

"You want the bookstore?" I asked, unable to focus on the conversation. I was still just so amazed and shocked that Dad had spoken with Abe. I wondered if he would have mentioned our fight. It seemed more impossible that he didn't. But maybe they had spoken after Dad had opened the letter but before we had fought. Could Abe know that I knew the truth about him being my father, not our dad, well, not his dad? I didn't listen as Abe talked about the bookstore. I got hot all of a sudden and left the office and wandered out through the books leaving him to talk to himself. There was an area at the end of one shelf where a nice comfortable chair was hidden away and I fell back into it.

Sitting there stressed, I took a few deep breaths. I did love this place, this store, but I could hardly imagine staying here forever, working here forever? I mean I always saw myself anywhere else, always searching, setting out on my own, creating, maybe even writing a book. I never imagined being here in town. My dad worked so much at the bookstore. He never seemed to mind because there was always one of us there with him, most of the time at least. We'd all worked there, but he never seemed to treat it like a family business, there was never talk about us joining him in running it. When Abe wanted to be a lawyer, Dad talked to him about Perry Mason. When Medi studied marketing it was never used as a tool to help the store, but whatever would make her happy. We were always taught to follow our dreams. I think that was why his anger and want for my help seemed so far flung out in left field.

The sun, bright across my face, disappeared as Abe came around the corner.

"Weren't we having a conversation?" he asked, crossing his arms and looking at me quizzically.

"Yeah, sorry, my head keeps spinning. What were we talking about?"

"I think the last thing you asked was 'Do you want the bookstore?' And my answer is yeah, I think I do. I'll have to talk to Mom and the rest of us, but I can't imagine anyone will try to stop me. I mean I know a lot of it, just growing up here. Dad told me a few things recently, people to talk to, the accountant, the bank manager. Folks like that. You've been working here these last couple months right?"

I shrugged, it was true I worked here full time when I first moved back. Dad had been sick, but once I got the job at the library I really started cutting back my time until I only stopped by on the odd weekday, if they needed help. "On and off."

He nodded, "Well, we'll talk about it later." Abe took a deep breath. "So, Henry…"

"What about Henry?" I asked, again more defensively than I meant to.

"Is it just me or does he look good?"

I burst out laughing. It was not what I expected from my quiet introverted brother. I smiled, feeling much lighter. "Yeah, he really does."

"He's aged well," he said, shaking his head and then reaching out his hand for me. Abe pulled me to my feet. "Let's go home."

11

SMOKING

Back at the house, we headed up the porch steps and I could hear raised voices. Abe went first and once the door opened I recognized Medi and her volume. You never knew what was annoying her, shoot, knowing my sister, she wasn't actually upset about anything, she was just being loud. I mean I couldn't blame her, my own emotions were crazy enough right then. Just before going inside I saw Llew standing on the driveway trying to get my attention. He was on the phone talking, but snapping and waving. I shrugged, but he only gestured more forcibly.

I let the door close behind Abe and headed across the yard. When I got close enough Llew gripped my wrist and then gave more attention to his phone since I was in his clutches.

"I appreciate it, you know I do-okay okay, it's just. Yeah-"

Llew started laughing and mimed tap dancing, pulling me around with him, while still giving all of his attention to the phone. I let him drag me around, this sort of thing was so normal for him, and I found myself appreciating it for the small fact that Llew didn't change. Little things like my brother's obnoxious traits were comforting. I didn't mind him commandeering my time, thankful to be on his schedule. Well, at least for the short term. I started to get bored with the fact that it didn't seem like I was caught up in the end of a phone call, but the middle or the beginning. I tried to pull my arm out of his grip, but he wasn't giving me an inch.

"Dude, Llew, Llew, Llewser, Llewellyn... let go, okay."

"Hold that thought Cat. What?" he said, seeming more annoyed with me and in turn making me shake my head. I probably looked both stunned and bemused.

"Let go of my wrist, and come get me when you're done with your phone call, okay."

"I'm almost done," he said as if bewildered by my actions.

"You're not almost done. I'm not going anywhere, release me, before I bite you."

Llew sighed dramatically and with narrowed eyes said into his phone, "Cat, I have to go, Lynman's being a brat."

"You fu-"

"Shhhhhh," he whispered, letting go of my wrist and laying a finger across my lips silencing me in the most condescending way possible. "I'll call you later."

He then made a flourish of hanging up the phone.

"You're such an asshole," I said.

"I love you," he responded and winked before slapping me heavily on the shoulder. "You want to smoke?" He pulled a joint out of his front pocket.

"No, I can't, you know that."

"Why can't you?"

"Because our mother will know, and I'll look crazy-"

"Crazier," he cut me off and lit up the joint. He slapped my shoulder one more time and in return I took hold of his arm and bit him with just enough force to leave the outline of my teeth.

"Shit," he said and shoved me safely away.

I pulled the pack of cigarettes out of my pocket and lit one up beside him.

"That's disgusting," he said and frowned.

"Not as disgusting as your face," I happily tossed back at him.

He pretended to perform a rimshot on invisible drums, at the same moment the front door opened, and we both automatically tried to jump out of view, not wanting to be caught. It turned out it was only Bennie. Llew and I laughed at our scare.

"Bennie-" Llew said.

"-Ben," I called.

"Old Bennie Kenobi!"

"Benji the hunted!"

"My favorite nephew come on over here," Llew demanded.

Bennie's face was a whirl of emotions, going from concern, to confusion, to relief. He walked down the steps and over to us, almost tripping on the curb, but Llew had stepped forward to let him bump safely against him.

Bennie smelled the air dramatically before Llew passed him the weed. "Bad influence," I whispered.

"It's better than what you've got," Bennie said.

"Burn," Llew added with a knowing smile.

"Yeah, yeah"

"It helps my glaucoma," Bennie joked.

"Just a baby toke for the baby," Llew said and ruffled Bennie's short hair.

Milo's raised voice could be heard coming through the back door, and Medi's matched it. It wasn't a happy discussion whatever it was.

"Let's go for a ramble," I said.

"Yes, please," Bennie answered, reaching out for another hit of Llew's pot and leading the way toward the cemetery.

"What's that about?" Llew asked.

"Who the fuck knows," Bennie said. I rarely hear my nephew cuss so I was a bit surprised. I was glad he was smiling and laughing with us, but I wanted to make sure he was alright.

"I imagine your mom just misses Grandpa," I said, hoping to comfort him.

"They've been fighting a lot lately, and it was before..." said Bennie, letting the sentence end unfinished, all of us knowing what he was about to say.

"That doesn't make sense, your mom only really likes to yell at me," Llew said smiling.

"Please, you never get yelled at," I cut in.

"It's because I'm perfect. Don't worry Benjamin. Your mom probably thought this was the right time to admit she's embezzling all that money from work, or she's fucking the milk man. One or the other?" he shrugged.

"Fuck, Llew," I said and breathed in the smoke wrong starting to cough. Bennie laughed, taking it as the joke it was meant to be. Of course I should have been well versed in my brother's inappropriate humor, but I suppose we'd been apart too long. I wanted to slap him, but he and Bennie were laughing so hard and looked so proud.

"The women in this family have no sense of humor," Llew said, making the desire to slap him even stronger.

I bared my teeth threateningly, and he pulled Bennie in front of him as a shield.

I almost wished I had a camera seeing the two of them together. They were a sight. Bennie had grown nearly as tall as Llew now. He had a beautiful mixed complexion of his parents, with my sister's freckles and her red hair lighting up his short tight curls. He was a great looking kid and I was surprised no one had scooped him up yet. Llew was looking almost as dark with his California tan. He had grown a bit of a beard and let his hair grow since we'd last seen each other, but I had watched it play out over pictures. His hair seemed lighter because of the sun. They both had my dad's nose and looked very much related laughing and passing the joint back and forth.

We wandered through the cemetery pointing out the names that made us laugh as kids. The Funk family, Mrs. Mildred Pitt, Rufus Pearl who we referred to as Rufus Hurl. We were ruthless but it wasn't our fault. I blamed Dad and I wasn't alone in it. Everyone called him Curtis, but his first name was really Lycurgus. He liked to complain often about why anyone would name a child Lycurgus. He called it cruel, but felt no guilt in passing on the pain and naming his children Abraham, Medi, Llewellyn and Emlyn, four names that weren't exactly Joe and Jane.

The best way to get on Llew's nerves was to call him by his proper name. It was something we did to violent outcomes as kids. Hardly anyone ever called me Emlyn, there was something aged or fragile sounding in the word that got under my skin, I was Lyn or Lynny to most and Lynman to my family. Henry always called me Em.

As we continued down the path we started up towards the playground, but before we got close I heard the sound of laughter that announced the teenage interlopers.

"Ugh," I moaned, and stopped walking.

"What?" Llew asked, before looking up at the playground.

"Bennie, who the fuck is that?" he said, hands on his hips "You have one job," he shouted dramatically with his realistic play anger, "one job to keep people out of our playground-"

"You do know, I don't live in this city."

"Carrying on the Newman name."

Bennie stuck out his hand, "Nice to meet you, Ben Washington."

"Well what are we going to do about this?" Llew asked, gesturing violently up the hill. "Lynman?"

"We could fuck them up," I said.

He nodded his head.

"That or we could go home and eat something. I'm fucking hungry," I said knowing the best way out of conflict.

"I saw a pie." Bennie said.

My brother sighed, his dramatic temper gone as quickly as it arrived.

"I suppose that settles it," Llew said, flipping the remnants of the joint into the trash can. "I could eat a whole pie."

12

MISSING

Mom was pulling the trashcans down to the curb when we arrived. "Oi, what are you doing Mom?" Llew shouted. "Let me get the trash."

"And steal my opportunity for some fresh air. You three seem like you've been enjoying the fresh air," she said pointedly.

"I'm so hungry," said Llew, ignoring motherly knowledge and rubbing his hands together. He snatched the trash can out of her grip and ran it down to the street.

Bennie disappeared into the house, while Mom and I waited on Llew. Once he was back she said, "Llew, you and Benjamin are sharing the guestroom tonight. I've put Abe in with you Lyn."

"Is Fletcher going to sleep between us?" I said not overly excited about sharing my room with my brother.

Mom frowned, "By the time Fletcher arrives, we'll have cleared out my studio, and one of you can be in there. Don't make a big deal. Your sister has practically been in tears over it."

"Over what?" I was confused.

"Oh, Milo feels like the three of them staying here is too much. I mean the house hardly has the space, but she really wants everyone here. So we're bunking up. It's good having you all around."

"Sure, sure," I said. "I'm just glad I'm not with Llew."

"Oh, we tried that, I'm sure you remember," Mom said and then turned to lead the way back inside.

Our house isn't too big, and luckily my parents had their children with enough time between them that the house never felt too crowded. Llew and I shared a room for close to a decade until our physical gymnastics started growing violent. We fought constantly for the front seat, the TV remote, who got to sit on the aisle at the movie theater. My mother was pretty good at ignoring us, but Dad would generally get angry. I said I would never forgive him the time he made me sit in the car instead of watching the movie, *Mission Impossible 2*.

I remember once diving around Llew's feet when he went to run up the stairs ahead of me for some race, but for my efforts I was kicked in the face and given a busted lip and a bloody nose. At the same time Llew fell face first into the stairs and was injured almost identically. Looking in the mirror we couldn't help but laugh. We laughed hysterically until Dad came in to see what was going on and when he saw us bleeding and swollen. He just shook his head and left the room.

Finally, they came to the decision to separate us just before I turned ten. One accident after another arose from jumping, tossing and falling from the top bunk bed in our room. We seemed to refuse to grow up and act right. The final straw was Llew trying to toss me from the bed into the clothes hamper we had filled with pillows. I missed the hamper, hit the window pane and broke my arm. The folks at the hospital seemed concerned enough by our series of accidents that an employee from child and family services came to talk to me. Dad seemed to believe we would end up dead or in jail if they didn't put a stop to us, and so they took apart the bunks and I was given Abe's bedroom long empty. It had stayed my room, pretty much ever since, though I knew if I argued Abe could always point out that it was his first.

The rest of the night was strangely joyous. We ordered pizza and ate in the kitchen that was brimming with people. The extra leaf was stuffed into the table and it reminded me of Thanksgiving. We all drank except Bennie, but I think he wasn't without his own joy supplied by Llew and their walk to take out the pizza boxes. There was only one thing missing from that night and he was felt in an amazing way. I was reminded of the children's nursery rhyme, *there was an old lady who lived in a shoe.* I knew that shoe. I recognized it. The shoe belonged to a giant, her husband, my father the giant. We lived in his shoe.

Dad was brought up often through the evening. Dad, who always added a mountain of Parmesan cheese to his pizza. Dad, who never ate his leftover pizza cold from the fridge but from the oven post warm up. Mom sat in Dad's chair that night at the table. She was the only one brave enough to do so and I was glad she did. We didn't have space to leave it empty, but I would have fought anyone else who got close. *I wish Dad was here,* was repeated enough times that you couldn't recall who said it last. Maybe no one said it; maybe it was the wine and the feelings playing like a record on repeat in my head.

Eventually, I stumbled off to bed, it wasn't too late, but I was drunk and trying to focus, trying to not let my brain spin too much. *Water and pain reliever,* I mumbled while I brushed my teeth. *Water and pain reliever,* I thought while I drank from the glass. *Water and pain reliever,* I whispered while I crawled under the covers. *I wish Dad was here,* I cried as I fell asleep.

13

TUESDAY, BUT NOT YET TUESDAY

I woke up feeling a little bit sick, a little bit hot, and a lot confused. Abe was in a heap on the far side of the bed under blankets. It's a big king sized bed so we were pretty far apart. I heard him snoring and I wiped the sweat off my face and neck. Laying there just for a few minutes I realized how shitty I felt and did the normal pledge to stop drinking, at least not to have more than a drink, two tops. Also, I reminded myself to be forgiving, at least this week.

Climbing out of the bed, I went into the bathroom. There I poured a large glass of water and sat on the edge of the tub to drink it. Abe's watch was next to the sink and I bent my neck to check the time. It was only just after one. I still felt a bit drunk, but at least I wasn't spinning anymore. I took a few more ibuprofen, and wandered with the water downstairs and out the front door.

It was too cold for pajama shorts and the holey t-shirt I was wearing, but I doubted I would be out too long. I just wanted to smoke. I was smoking a lot these days as well. I needed to stop. "Soon," I whispered to the darkness. I left the property and walked just over to the low stone fence at the end of the dead end which ran at a right angle between our house and the Hayden's. I stepped awkwardly, feeling every piece of gravel under my bare feet, and was relieved to sit on the frigid stone that was lining the lane. The front porch light was on at our house. I could tell the small light above the kitchen sink was on too. It was the normal night lights. Everyone in the house, even Milo and Bennie had slept here enough to know where the piano bench stuck out, and were sure not to trip or stub a toe on the heavy sculptures that my mother turned into doorstops.

I traded off drinking the water and smoking the cigarette, shivering into the wind.

"Can-"

"SHIT," I half shouted. I was caught completely off guard by Henry who appeared right beside me, "Christ, Hank."

"I'm sorry," he said smiling. "That's what you get for sitting out here, next to a graveyard in the middle of the night, you're already set up for a scare."

"My brain's a bit foggy right now." I said and shivered again against the weather.

"Here, put this on," he said, shaking his head and pulling his striped wool sweater off before passing it to me.

"I'm alright," I said, but put the cigarette down and pulled the heavy material over my head anyway. I realized how nice it smelled, so much like Henry, snug and inviting. It brought his warmth. I started to reach for my smoke.

"Don't burn the sweater please," he said. He hated my smoking. I tried not to do it when he was around, but he caught me off guard that night.

I shook my head and tossed the cigarette on the ground and declared, "Safe."

His smile faltered for a moment, he scratched the back of his head before sitting down beside me. My knee touched his and stopped feeling so cold. I don't believe it had much to do with the sweater, or his shared heat. Next to me, Henry said, "I'm sorry Em."

"You have every right to want to protect this beauty. I know you've seen my old burnt up hoodie."

"No, I mean about Curt. He was a good, kind man. He and your mom always made me feel like family."

I looked away from him then, it's not like I hadn't been talking or thinking about Dad all day, but for some reason I didn't want to talk or think about him with Henry, not now, all I wanted was to be distracted by his sweater and the press of denim.

"What was the movie?"

"The movie?" he asked, confused.

I watched the breath flit free between his lips and found myself staring at his mouth. I wanted a closer look. I meant to ask about the movie he mentioned at the library yesterday, and it hit me, my god, could it have really only been yesterday? I was probably still drunk. I didn't want to think about my dad and instead I leaned closer to his breath and his lips and tried to kiss him.

Tried, that is the word that marked the moment. I leaned in and Henry pulled up, so if my eyes were closed my aim would have eventually landed directly on his collar.

"Em," he said quietly, but not in the way that I wanted him to say my name, not loving or wanting; instead, it was just sort of sad.

"I know this isn't the right way or moment, but you know, life is short. That's what I'm supposed to take away from this-"

"Em," he said again, cutting me off.

"I think I'm in love with you. I mean, not think, I know I am." I started realizing this wasn't going as it should, but I meant it, all of it.

"Please, you don't want to do this now. Not while everything is hurting. Take it from me," he said and stood up.

Just the act, the distance he put between us. Me, an island declaring my love; me, who tried, tried and failed to kiss him. My heart fell into my stomach and the ill feeling of the hangover returned and every bad moment from the last 36 hours. Yesterday, I had so much. One mistake after the other and I just kept losing things. How could I stop this? In some corner of my brain something shouted, *you killed your father!* I had to face it. I didn't deserve this love, not now that was for sure. All I wanted to do was run away, maybe hop on my motorcycle and drive far away, but I couldn't even do that. I had promised Mom I wouldn't and so I was stuck. My head throbbed and Henry was talking, but whatever he said I didn't hear it. I stood up, shaking off his words.

"Emlyn," he said, using my whole name, his voice rising. He tried to take my hand, but I jerked it back violently.

"Forget it," I said and stumbled backward against the stone fence, barely keeping on my feet. "Please, forget all of it."

I turned then and walked into the house, unable to look back. I climbed the steps, rising up to the second floor and realizing I had forgotten the water glass outside, but I did have the sweater. I tore it off and tossed it into the corner, before crawling back into bed. It took me a long moment to realize Abe was still where I left him; still snoring.

14

ROUGH MORNING

"Hey . . . Lynman."

A hand rocked my shoulder, and I forced one eye open. The world was foggy and I wrestled my arm from beneath my body and pulled off my headphones that were starting to choke me.

Abe laughed to himself. "You look about as good as I feel."

"I'm still young right? I just don't know when it happened," I croaked. "For a brief moment in time I could drink anything, stay up all night. Fuck. Why am I awake?"

"Your sister calls."

"What?"

"Medi came up, she wants you two to go shopping."

"Oh yeah," I groaned. I remembered at some point over pizza we decided to go buy something to wear for the viewing and funeral. I didn't have anything appropriate or comfortable enough for all the days ahead.

"You alright?" Abe asked.

Though he said he felt terrible he looked fine. He still had the resting sad look that I think we all were carrying right now without much control over our facial muscles.

"Sure," I said, "I'm as fine as any of us are." This was a lie of course. I wasn't fine. Just looking at him made me wonder things I never wondered before. Did he think about me only as a sister? Did he ever think about me and how life could have been different for both of us? The guilt of these thoughts made me want to shake myself. I had one father, only one father and he was dead. I had helped make him that way. And Henry, how was I going to face Henry again.

Abe looked like he wanted to say something, but I didn't let him.

"I'm going to take a shower," I announced before loudly and slowly groaning my way through the room.

The shower helped me wake up a bit, but I couldn't stop thinking about Henry, and how in the world I was going to deal with him. Maybe I could drown myself, I thought for a few minutes letting the hot water run into my mouth, swishing it around since I hadn't brushed my teeth yet. I leaned against the wall thinking I could stay there all day, wondering how long until I was missed.

I suppose, I should have been happy, having something new to worry about to split with the loss of my father. I could switch from one terrible thing to the next. I started to cry in the shower for a minute but it was just too melodramatic, the realization causing me to laugh with slight hysterics before I pulled myself back to center.

I forced myself to keep it together while I got dressed, though I could feel how close I was to losing it. With just a little push I would be sobbing again. I was thankful that Abe was gone when I passed through the room. I saw the colorful sweater from last night on the floor and took a moment to pick it up and lay it neatly across the back of the chair.

Outside of my room I heard voices coming from every direction. It seemed like I was the last to rise that day. From the yard, Mom and Abe were chatting, in the living room my sister talked with her husband and son. I crept and didn't see anyone until I got to the kitchen. Sitting at the kitchen table Llew was looking rough. He was leaning over a cup of coffee and he yawned a giant mirror to my own pausing gasp. We both looked at each other and started to shake our heads.

"Morning sunshine," he muttered, and handed me his coffee mug. I drained all that he had left before pouring him a refill and getting my own mug. There was a cold pizza in the fridge and I pulled it open and tossed it in the center of the table. "I already ate," he said, but before I took my second bite he joined in.

"So last night," he kept on.

I mumbled an affirmative.

"Yeah, last night. I drank a lot," he said and smiled.

"I think that was the theme of the evening. I'm going to try not to drink so much tonight otherwise they might as well put me in the coffin too."

"I'm going to be cremated," he stated.

"I'll snort you in the funeral home bathroom," I mumbled.

He started laughing hard, half shocked that I was the one who said it and as if it was the funniest thing he'd ever heard. He held his throbbing head and continued to laugh.

"Too loud," I muttered, and he covered his mouth apologetically.

I ignored him and picked up the open newspaper. I looked at the page it was open to and was immediately attentive when I realized sitting there was my dad's obituary. I snatched the paper up and started to read it.

Lycurgus Mitchell Newman, 65, died Sunday, October 10th after a prolonged illness. He was born in New Carlisle on March 7, 1954 to Mitchell and Janet Newman. He is survived by his wife, Susan and their four children.

"What the hell is this?" I was shocked at such a short obit.

Llew was still catching his breath, but managed to glance my direction and see what I was talking about.

"Oh you know the ole *Four Caster*'s obituary. It's pretty lame. Probably written by some college credit earning intern."

"This is a fucking travesty, I mean Dad's store is a town landmark. He had an amazing life. I mean what is this, three sentences? Three goddamned sentences."

"Calm down Lynman, nobody reads this shit anymore."

"It's bullshit," I said, pissed off.

Llew opened his mouth to say what, I don't know, but in the end he couldn't, because at that moment Medi walked in, purse on her arm.

"Ready?" she asked.

"Yeah, let's go," I said and stood up to leave. I hated how angry I was. I mean I felt it was suitable, my anger. Just a generic few words to try and encapsulate his life, yet Llew didn't deserve that. It was too early for shouting. I shook it off, hoping a change of scenery would do me good.

15

SISTERS

Shopping at the mall on a Tuesday morning is a bit odd. I mean in general I think malls are weekend places. Well, I suppose if I'm speaking frankly, malls are truly things of the past, but I do have good memories there. Growing up, it was the sort of spot you could go to as a family but be sure to move in separate orbits for the day. We would wander from pet stores, to record stores, and on to the arcade which my mother strangely seemed to fear. I don't know what she thought went on in the arcade, maybe drug deals? Gang recruitments? Sex beneath the pinball machines? I miss the overlapping sounds and flash of neon. All those places are gone now, and the mall is half ghost town, but not entirely dead yet. There are a number of different clothing stores, so at least if you don't find what you want at one place you have a chance to get it somewhere else.

Medi and I have different tastes. She was looking for a dress, something classy and sleek. I'm sure she'll look gorgeous; she always does. I found myself looking for something I could build on and maybe subconsciously wear for other days. Skirts, sweaters, shirts, pants, you know, layers. The Macy's store was practically empty that morning. The turnstiles of clothes were inviting, tall enough that I could duck and disappear if I wanted to, but instead I could see Medi's head bob above the racks. She found me soon after with arms full of black material. I had just a couple things that seemed to pale in comparison, and that was literal, as I started to wonder if the colors I picked out were truly even black.

"Do you want help?" she asked.

I shook her off with a sigh and a few words. "Still just browsing," I said as if there were a hundred first choices to pick between.

"They have a great collection, just over there. I think you should take a look."

"Thanks," I mumbled. She disappeared and as much as I hated it, I did go over where she had been shopping. I walked between the clothing, shoving things that insulted me with their trendy cuts and overt style. Nothing makes me as angry as an extra-large bow.

I was close to being done with the whole thing. Thinking that maybe I could wear a black tracksuit, or something equally embarrassing. Yet it was at that moment when I saw a plain black dress, minus capes, lace, ruffles or any other hideous addition. It had the length I wanted without being something a grandmother from the Victorian age would rock. Flipping between the sizes, things were even better when mine was actually there. Hopefully, it would look good.

I took it off the rack and went to head over to the dressing room. I was almost there when I heard my name.

"Emlyn Newman," a random voice called to me. It's strange to be recognized out in the middle of nowhere.

I looked back and with near horror noticed one of the everyday patrons of the library trying to get my attention, at least she hadn't snapped her fingers. Mrs. Pearson was the type of person who felt like she owned the library and treated us as if we were all her servants. She complained about a book or newspaper that spent more than five minutes left where they were laid. She hated the romance novels with their bodice ripping covers, or the happy sounds of children from the story hours. She shouted at all of us in loud voices if we didn't refer to her as ma'am, and was shocked and disgusted if we didn't know everything about every book in the collection.

"Playing hooky I see. Off at the mall instead of at your job. I'm curious if the library knows where you are, Miss Newman."

"Ma'am I do believe they know where I am, or at least where I'm not," I said, oddly enough wishing I was at the library. At least at the library we had built a system to save each other with false phone calls, safe words, and fanciful emergencies when pinned by Mrs. Pearson. In this situation I could be trapped for goodness knew how long. One of the hardest parts of my job was dealing with people who seemed to believe the customer was always right. Polite customers were more often right than rude entitled ones if you ask me.

"Well, I imagine we'll see. I plan on stopping back by on my way home. My holds should be available. As long as you put the request in when I asked. I just don't understand what could possibly be taking so long. If they aren't there when I stop by I'm going to give the director a call, because it has really been a ridiculous wait."

"Things take time Mrs. Pearson, and we can't control how quickly books are read or how long people keep them even after they are due."

I would have turned into a black hole if given a chance. I felt the deep desire to just walk away. Some folks never seemed to understand that my life wasn't my job. When I wasn't there, I didn't think about any parts of the library. Well, maybe the books, I could think about my own personal relationship with stories all day long, but the Mrs. Pearsons of the world could take a flying leap.

"I think at the next library council meeting I'm going to bring this type of thing up. I mean it's really ridiculous and inconsiderate. There are no deterrents from just taking the books, and you all seem to care nothing about us taxpayers."

"We do have fines, and policies around this type of thing. I promise people are not allowed just to take the books."

I could tell she was getting ready to go on another speech about the laziness of the staff, or how the world was ending, but at that moment, Medi came out of the dressing room.

"Well, I think I have my dress. I want your opinion though."

Mrs. Pearson looked at Medi as if she was a fly to wave away, and treated her as such. "Excuse me young lady but we were having a conversation."

All of a sudden my heart took a hopeful swing, because the look on Medi's face was priceless. She didn't know this woman but she seemed to recognize that this woman certainly didn't know her either. Though my sister might be hurt by a sharp word from her family. Her career had taught her to be ruthless at times, and unless you shared blood or a marriage license, you didn't step to my sister.

"Mrs. Pearson, I'd like to introduce you to my sister Medi Washington. Medi, this is one of the library's patrons Mrs. Pearson." I think my sister must have noticed my hassled face. As much as I complained, there were some situations where having an older pushy sibling was great and I could tell this might be one of them. Mrs. Pearson on the other hand didn't seem to notice.

"Charmed, as I was saying about the committee-"

"I'm sorry," Medi interrupted, "are you working today Lyn?"

"No-"

"Perhaps Mrs. Pearson, I could get your opinion about something else? These dresses for instance, what do you think? You see, my sister and I are here shopping for dresses to wear to our father's funeral. He died on Sunday, and I believe whatever petty concerns that you have about library business and committees is pretty inappropriate. So if you'll excuse us, why not go to the library and fill out a comment card, because we have our own business in which to attend." Medi pulled me away at that moment, and back toward the dressing room.

The look on Mrs. Pearson's face was one of shock and terror. I couldn't tell what part seemed to appall her most but just the thought gave me the jolt of energy I was missing. The way Medi had said, 'go to the library' could have easily been translated as 'go to hell' and I was truly living for the moment.

"God, that was great, thank you," I said to Medi, smiling broadly.

"I can't believe you even let her. You should have stood up for yourself. Truthfully, I don't know why you're working at the library, from what I see, and what you say, it's not what you wanted. I know you think everything I say is dumb, but I know you were happier at the store with Dad. I mean at least at the store it's our rules, you don't have to kowtow to the uppity bitches of the world."

Almost as quickly as I was happy, Medi was Medi again and trying to mother me, but I pushed it aside. I was just happy to have moved past that encounter.

"Let me see your dress," she said. She cocked her head back and forth before accepting it. "Okay, that will look great, once we get you a pair of shoes."

Once again she was right.

"Fashion show," I said like we used to as kids before disappearing into my room to change. The dress was good. It wasn't something I would probably ever wear again, so it wasn't what I planned, but it would work for the funeral and viewing. I slipped on one of the black sweaters I had considered as well and realized I could pull it on to add a little bit of variety from one day to the next. I left the dressing room at almost the same moment as Medi. We were different enough that it was hard to tell we were related. She was tall with red hair and fair skin. She and Llew took after our mom in their hair coloring, well Llew's beard at least, is red. His hair is usually darker though it seems to change with how much sun is around. Abe and I have dark brown hair like Dad. Growing up and thinking I was adopted, it was always a happy coincidence. I was the knock off version of my parents, curls like Mom and dark-haired like Dad. Now, it seemed like it made more sense, the genetic knock off, not just by chance.

The dress was good though, Medi and I both commented on it. It fell straight, hiding the curves I wanted to hide, but helping to show off a few others. I tried to remind myself it was a funeral. I didn't need to look great, but I would happily settle for good. It was nice to know I wasn't going to wear that track suit. Medi of course looked stunning.

"You look beautiful," I said, while she still seemed to be deciding in the mirror.

"Thanks," she replied. "Might as well look good, since I'm just going to be sobbing the whole time. You're so lucky, keeping your emotions under control. For me, once I start sobbing, fuck it."

"Don't worry about it, your father only dies once," I said. "I'm glad you, Milo and Bennie are at the house." I wasn't sure if I meant it, but she had done me a kindness and I wanted to pay her back.

"Thank you for saying that. Milo has just been driving me crazy these days. I mean we're family. You should be with family during times like this. How hard is that to understand? Sometimes, I feel like I hardly know him."

"Oh, you know him. It's got to be hard on Milo. He doesn't really have a relationship with his father, does he?"

"No, they're like two positive magnets, you try to put them together and they do all they can to push the opposite way. I try to get them to talk and work through things, but he's afraid of getting hurt if you ask me."

"Poor Milo," I said. My brother-in-law was the type of guy that you just really wanted to be happy, to have the perfect life. He was so kind and laid back. He was walking bedside manner. He made everything better when he was around.

"Poor Milo? At least Milo has a chance to fix things with his father. I was bitching at Dad last week. You know how he could be. Every decision I made he seemed to see the fault in it. He was such a worrier. It's where you get it. I wish I could take that frustration back."

"Yeah," I agreed, but I didn't say more. I didn't want to tell her about the fight Dad and I had that day. I didn't want to tell her that it was my fault we didn't have a father anymore. I don't think she would have held anything against me. Medi was forgiving of her family, but at the same time, I couldn't let her feel bad for me. I couldn't give her another opportunity to want to take care of me.

"Henry understands. I'm so lucky that we've stayed close all this time. Sometimes and never repeat this, but I wonder what my life would be like if I had stayed in a relationship with him. I mean everything would be different, but at least it would be easy. Things seemed to make sense with Henry. You remember how happy he and I were together, right?"

"Well, sure, but you and Milo are happy?" I said not wanting to hear this stuff, not wanting to ask questions that would delve deeper into my sister's relationships then and now.

"Don't get married Lynny. I tell you. The person you become is so different from the person you once were. I think when I see Henry, I just see the young and happy girl I was in pig-tails. The girl, who still had her daddy. I understand why people have affairs."

"Really, why?"

"Why?" she parroted back.

"Why do people have affairs?"

She shrugged, but answered, "to escape the life they have."

I walked back into the dressing room once she said that. I didn't want to hear more about my sister and Henry and affairs. I knew she wasn't having one. I was certain I would know. It was one of the reason's Llew's joke yesterday was so ridiculous, but another part of me wondered if maybe Medi wasn't alone in her daydreams. Maybe Henry was enjoying the time he was spending with my sister these days. There were so many reasons he could have stopped me last night. Just the idea of being stuck in a love triangle with my sister was enough to make me feel nauseous.

"Okay, these dresses work. Let's go find those shoes," Medi called from back in her own dressing room.

"Sounds like a plan," I whispered to myself while feeling the continuing weight of these days.

16

PICTURES

"Look at Abe's hair," said Llew as he held up an old favorite of my brother. The hair in question is long, with the childhood curls that disappeared too late for Abe's liking, giving my oldest brother nearly an afro. Dressed in a hockey jersey, he's ignoring the camera with his eyes directed to something out of sight. We all recognize the room where it's taken, and so we know he's watching the TV, but what's playing is anyone's guess. Abe has single handedly led a campaign to make these pictures disappear over the years, but the rest of us all do everything we can to protect them.

"God," Abe mumbles, "please give me that."

"Never," I say.

"Yeah it's going in the display," Llew declares.

We were going through pictures. There was going to be a slideshow as well as framed shots around the room where tomorrow's viewing would be held. I doubt we'll really include this picture of Abe since Dad's nowhere to be seen, but it's the type of joke I appreciate and so I agree wholeheartedly.

"I've got Abe's 8th grade class photo up in my room, I really think Dad would want that one to help open the slideshow. I mean really, what screams Dad more than a weird white boy flat-top."

"Hey you two," said Abe and then flips us the bird. Llew acts wounded. I just laughed.

My brother had a pretty great transformation I must say. I think it took him a long time to figure things out, he was a mess of 80s fashion and experimental haircuts a lot of his childhood. So many of these pictures catch him in what feels like a never ending awkward phase. It wasn't until he left home and went away to school that the Abe who I knew was created. Studying at Dashell was huge, not only was he blessed with school uniforms and policy, but he was able to meet different people from different places, far from the strong personalities of my family. Of course I don't know the Abe from before I was born; and the one from after was someone I got to know at holidays or special occasions, so the meticulous, specific and determined Abe feels so different from the one in pictures and my parent's recollections. It gives me joy to consider.

We moved to a picture of Llew and I as tots. I notice my own curls that I realize for the first time were inherited from Abe. Llew leaned over and looked at the picture. "Was it just me, or was I really cute?"

"Pretty cute, but you had a big head," I replied pointing at his truly normal-sized noggin.

"Hmmmm, I wonder if I had a kid if it would have that skull?"

"Fifty-fifty chance I imagine. Just make sure you make babies with a small-headed woman."

Llew pondered this idea, nodded, and we kept at it.

The picture search became the theme of the afternoon. It turned into a family event and everyone piled into the front room sitting around the coffee table to go through these pictures. Mom was happy to narrate some of the earlier events and we were sure to be cruel to each other's clothing and haircuts. It was a lot of fun choosing the pictures we liked the most.

I saw Bennie sitting back in one of the chairs and using his phone to magnify the newspaper in his hand.

"Don't bother B," I said, knowing he was looking at the obituary page. "I don't know who wrote that shitty obit, but it's a real joke."

Llew sighed deeply across the room, where he was pouring a drink. "Not this again."

I looked around the room and saw some confusion on everyone's face. "Have you all seen it? It's ridiculous."

My mom shook her head. "It's the standard obit for the paper darling. It's not *David Copperfield* I'll give you, but I'm glad they spelled his name right."

Everyone laughed and I just shook my head. I don't know why this became the hill I planned to die on, but it felt important to me.

"It's pretty funny, that you care," Llew added, "you being adopted and all." He laughed at the old joke. Ever since we found out I was adopted, it became Llew's line. Anytime I had a different opinion than the rest, *it's because you're adopted.* Whenever I excelled at something, *it's because you're adopted.* Anytime we tried to decide whose turn it was to ask if we could go to the party, or order out for dinner, *it makes sense for you to ask, they won't say no, because you're adopted.*

It was a Llew joke; it was nothing new, nothing that should have bugged me, but something about hearing it that day, while my brain was fried, exhausted and wrestling over every emotion in the emotion box, it made something flip. Without a word, I took hold of the heavy ceramic coaster on the side table next to me and winged it at my brother's face. It struck the wall just inches from Llew's head and the room erupted.

"What the fuck-"

"It was just a joke."

"You could have really hurt him-"

"Llewellyn are you alright?"

"Well, it wasn't that funny."

"Lynman-"

"Everyone calm down."

"Is it broken?"

"Your brother-"

"No," I stopped them angrily. "Not my brother, because I'm adopted, remember?"

Everyone started speaking then, talking on top of each other, trying to smooth things over, but I didn't want to calm down, or deal with them at that moment. I just wasn't in the mood for my family. I needed some air and space and so I walked through the room and out the front door.

17

SECRETS

Outside, it felt like a perfect day. The light wasn't too bright. The sky was blue and around me the trees were changing colors. I headed over the stone fence and up into the cemetery the same as I always did when I needed to get away from my family. I was halfway up the hill, when I heard someone say my name. Glancing back over my shoulder I saw Abe trailing behind.

"Are you winded?" I asked, seeing him put his hands behind his head to catch his breath.

"You were walking really fast, shut up."

"What do you want?" I said snippier than he deserved, but at the same time feeling I had left for a reason.

"I want to talk to you, okay?"

I sighed deeply, but as long as it was only him, I could deal with it. I gestured over to a bench, under a tree and while we walked over I pulled out a cigarette.

Once we got situated, I felt better, calmer. I knew it was stupid, but I was just so rattled. If I was a boat I would be close to capsizing.

"You know he didn't mean it?" Abe said cautiously, saying something we both knew to be true, but not something that he was sure would be easy for me to hear.

"Yeah of course, he can just be such an ass."

Abe laughed, "Yup."

We were silent for a minute, looking out across the peaceful grounds before he went back to talking.

"I'm not going to disagree with you. I just thought we were all used to it by now." Abe probed, but I didn't respond and after a moment he followed up. "You want to talk about it?"

"Talk about what?" I shrugged.

"Everything that's bothering you. I know that you and Dad had a fight that last day. I hope you're not carrying that around?"

"If only you knew," I said.

"Try me," said Abe. I felt him pleading.

I laughed a bit sadly, but couldn't bring myself to talk about it. Even if this seemed like the door I was looking for, the perfect opportunity to spill it all out on the table, but I was a chicken. I just couldn't. I shook my head slowly and took a long drag on my smoke before I said anything.

"It's nothing, it's everything, it's a lot of things."

"Nothing, everything, Henry?"

I glanced up quickly, too quickly to be able to smoothly deny it. Still, I didn't say anything, but Abe didn't seem to need it.

"Yesterday, you hardly seemed able to look him in the eye and then magically I wake up this morning to see the sweater he was wearing flung across the desk chair in your bedroom. Not to mention the face you make every time his name gets mentioned the last few days," Abe squinted quizzically at me while he made this statement. "Oh, and the fact that you've been in love with him practically your whole life."

I really have to hand it to Abe. He was talking about faces, but the one I must have made once he said that was certainly unique, a mix of horror and embarrassment that could have been marketed as a Halloween mask, yet somehow he didn't laugh.

"I don't . . . how? No," I verbally stumbled, and Abe smiled kindly at this new anxiety he caused, seeming to think it was for the best.

"Oh you're right it's my other sister," he said and then he really laughed, "bad choice of words."

I started to bury my head in my hands, but he caught my grip and held on to it.

"It's ridiculous, there's nothing there," I said defensively. "I mean it would be weird with Medi, shoot for all I know, she's still in love with him."

Abe rolled his eyes. "Last time I checked, Medi has a husband."

"Yeah, but they fight."

"Lynman, do you want me to call you next time Fletch and I get into it? If you're lucky you won't have to wait long since he's coming up in the morning. When you're together awhile, you find yourself in fights over folding laundry, takeout, or the volume of a sneeze. It's an amazing and a rather odd thing that moment when you get comfortable enough to show someone all that's inside of you, all that mess. It doesn't mean you don't love someone. It means the opposite I think."

I shook my head.

"I think you'll feel better if you do something."

"Yeah, well I tried something. I tried something last night and I do not feel better. In fact, I feel like a right asshole."

Abe frowned thinking it over but his attention shifted because from our place on the bench we saw Medi and Llew step over the stone wall and start up the hill towards us. Medi waved with a big smile, Llew seemed more cautious. It was a bit funny, him so tall, towering over Medi, but being led. I didn't know if he was going to be mad at me. History favored his forgiveness, but we'd had lingering fights before. I sighed deeply, knowing I couldn't run from my brother and my family any longer.

Hearing me sigh, Abe put his arm around my shoulder and jostled me just enough to make me scowl. "You know what they say right?" he asked.

"What do they say Abraham?"

"If at first you don't succeed," he looked at me hopefully, but didn't finish the sentence.

"If at first you don't succeed... Do you have another coaster?"

Abe laughed before saying, "No, that's not what I mean, who I mean."

Medi and Llew were growing close enough to hear most of our words now so he whispered in my ear. "Talk to Henry again. Don't give up."

Across from us, Medi untangled from Llew and stuck out her hand for Abe, "Come on, you can push me on the swing."

Abe took her hand and the two of them swung their joined grip up and down, like overgrown kids. At the last minute, Medi looked back at us, "You two be good, alright. No hitting."

"Lynman started it," Llew shouted and sat hard on the bench, making my side lift up slightly before settling back down. "I hate when she does that. We're not little kids," he grumbled. "She's so bossy."

"Yeah," I agreed, but didn't know what else to say.

"You didn't start it, I actually started it. I didn't mean it, you know. I shouldn't have said that, even though it was just a joke. A bad joke."

"I know, and it's like ninety-nine times out of a hundred I would have laughed it off, but today I freaked out. Maybe I'm being hormonal or something. Maybe-"

"Maybe your dad just died," he said.

I sighed pushing off the urge to cry and focused on Llew.

"I'm glad I didn't hurt you. Gosh, that would have made a bad week worse."

Llew lifted his giant hand and slapped me gently with it, before pulling me close and kissing my cheek. We settled into each other comfortably, but I glanced up and could see his face. He frowned darkly with sadness and my heart hurt to see it.

"I keep waiting to stop being such a screw up, you know. Every year, I think it'll just stop. This is the year I say the right things and actually turn into a full-fledged adult."

"Fuck it, it's stupid and it's hard," I said.

"It is, right? It's fucking hard." He took a deep breath. "Can I tell you a secret?"

"Yeah, of course."

"Cat's pregnant."

My eyes went wide hearing these words. I was sure that of all my siblings, Llew was the furthest from having kids, even further in wanting them. It was a definite shock.

"Oh wow," I said, happy with that response. Glad it wasn't negative, just a surprise.

"Right? Oh wow." He moved off the bench, sitting heavily at my feet. He pulled out a handful of grass and tore it apart.

"You know what?" I said.

"What?" said Llew.

"You're going to be a great dad," I answered and realized I meant it. I took a deep clear breath of fresh air and nodded with confidence.

"I'm sorry, are you high?" he replied, raising his eyebrows incongruently.

"I mean, it's something you have to learn, but you're the most fun person I know. As long as you don't try and lower the baby out the window in a laundry basket," I said smiling. In all truth that was something I tried to do to him. He made it about ten feet from the ground, when I misjudged the remainder of the space and dropped him. The sound that came out of him was enough to make me start packing a bag.

"God, we were dumb," he said smiling.

"But we sure were fun," I replied. "It's a good thing we tried out so many stupid things, that way you'll know how not to toss a baby. Is Cat excited?"

"She's over the moon. I think she's a bit sad that I didn't ask her to come with me. I probably should have invited her."

"You still could," I said.

"You think?"

"Fletcher's not coming until tomorrow. I don't know about work, but you could always stay an extra day, I'm sure Mom would love to meet her."

"She cried that she didn't get to meet Dad," he said and shook his head. "That's something isn't it?"

I only swallowed hard with only a nod as my answer. I understood nonetheless.

"Okay, your turn," he said.

"My turn to what, have a baby, no I d-"

"Tell me a secret," he said, cutting me off.

Without a pause or a promise of secrecy, without a single thought checking my mouth before it opened, I said, "Well, I found out Abe's my real father and then I went and told Dad I knew, which is probably the reason he died."

Llew looked at me speechless, which was such a new expression for him. It would have been fun to point out later, if only this was a conversation I had planned to relive.

"Well shit," he finally managed. "I have so many questions. How? Who?"

"I have so few answers, but Brynn and I got stoned over the weekend. She told me."

"And you remembered?"

I laughed, "No, I wrote myself a little note."

"What did Dad say?"

"Nothing much, just that he was my real father and he loved me. I mean, I didn't throw a fit or anything and thank god I told him I loved him back, but I shouldn't have done that Llew," my voice cracked. I wanted to take it back so badly.

"It's crazy, but don't be an idiot and think you killed him."

"It was the same day Llew, how is that a coincidence?"

"Look, do you know how many years I probably stole from the old man. The time I wrecked Scott Kidd's motorcycle, or when I got picked up for spray painting the football field. If we're placing blame, I'm sure Dad would have lived another good five years if it wasn't for me. Don't steal all the attention. I had a real strong hand in weakening the old man's heart."

Strangely this helped. I couldn't blame Llew for his hellion days, for all the bad behavior he got into and how it might have led us to this moment, so a part of the weight I was carrying felt lighter as well.

"You make things better," I said as a way of thanks and he scoffed a laugh.

"So," Llew asked, "who knows that you know?"

"You," I responded.

"Only me?"

"Yeah, Brynn I'm sure thinks I don't remember, and I really don't. I have no idea how it came up, or where it came from. I don't know if I'll ever mention it to Mom or Abe, or anyone else."

"To think, Abe a fucking father. It's all so weird. It makes sense though. You and him both get all antsy and get in that pretzel position, when you're uptight."

I was crossing my arms right then but uncrossed them long enough to punch Llew.

He climbed to his feet, dumping handfuls of grass on me as he stood.

I followed him up, and shook back and forth like a dog coming in from the rain. Once I stopped moving he pulled me into a bone crushing hug. "Favorite," he whispered to me, a word we used since childhood to denote the other. "Favorite," I answered back.

18

DEVILISH WAYS

We went to join Medi and Abe, and I was surprised to see them not up at the playground, but instead standing down the hill from our swings. It was easy to see why though since the loud laughter, intermixed with bits of foul language showed the teens seemed back claiming their space.

"Hooligans," Llew said, with enough sincerity that I started to laugh. "When did this happen?" he demanded.

"Hooligans? Do you mean when did you turn into a 50s TV cop?"

He glared at me.

"Or do you mean, when did a public playground become used by the public?"

"It's always been a public playground, but no one except us ever used it," he said truthfully.

"Eh, I'm not sure. Maybe kids are braver with the cemetery. No imagination of night goblins like we were. It's sort of nice to see them out and about though, instead of on computers."

Llew gave me a disgusted look and scoffed. "That library has ruined you."

"If you're not careful I'm going to ruin you," I replied.

He rolled his eyes and shoved me off the path and into a trashcan.

"I mean, is school even out yet?"

I glanced at my watch and saw it was closer to dinner time then school, but only shrugged.

"Delinquents," I muttered.

"Before I leave we're going to figure this out," he said more to him-self than to me. It made me laugh how much sharing the playground bothered him. The kids had been there on and off since I moved home. I did a lot of walking through the cemetery, but in general I found myself heading in different directions knowing the playground might be occu-pied. I missed having a place like that for myself, so I admit it frustrated me, but it was at the bottom of the list of things to concern myself over. War with local children could wait until things were better and life more boring.

"Friends again?" Medi asked when we finally caught up to them.

"Hardly," I said.

"What with her? She smells like a trashcan."

Medi ignored us. "I feel a group hug coming on, a Newman family hug."

Though when she got a good look at me she changed her train of thought.

"Lyn you have grass in your hair," she said, but before she could try to clean me up Llew stepped between us.

"Bring it in, Mrs. Washington," Llew said, and reached wider to pull both Abe and I into the mix as well.

"Don't you call my sister that," I said with my head comfortably tucked against soft cotton. "Hugs not over until Llew licks Abe."

Llew tried to grab Abe, but he seemed ready for it and jumped away and ran down the hill and back towards the house with Llew on his heels. Medi and I smiled at each other and then laughed before heading back home.

I tried to walk back with my head held high so I wouldn't arrive like a kid called back to the dinner table after a tantrum and lucky for me, as we walked up to the door it was the same moment that my Uncle Amos's old town car pulled up. Uncle Amos and Brynn climbed out. They were going to stay the next two nights with us. It would make the house even tighter, but I couldn't help but be happy to see them. Brynn was always the third musketeer to Llew and I growing up. She could easily cause enough trouble that it was impossible to know who was to blame. She was raised alone with her father, my uncle, who was one of my favorite people in existence. With long gray curls and a long mustache he looked like he was transported out of some western. He seemed to follow that odd, out of time and place, theme with old suits that seemed a size too large but were his signature look.

Uncle Amos was a history teacher and a writer of nonfiction type books. He could fill up the whole afternoon with whatever subject he was becoming an expert on that season and usually it was something I would find just as interesting. Sure he was a bit eccentric, sometimes forgetting to shave part of his face, losing his keys every time he visits and starting or ending conversations you are only halfway through, but he brightens a room just by being there.

"There are my girls," he said, seeing Medi and I. We received our scratchy hugs that lasted longer than normal as a way to show his emotion. It was because of Amos that Mom and Dad met. He was friends with Dad first. The two of them were known to talk hours after the rest of us went to sleep, pouring through old books and trying to remember what they had wanted to say, for hours on end their conversations would linger.

Llew popped out the door, with everyone else trailing him.

"Here are our travelers," Amos barked.

We spent the next twenty minutes milling around the yard, talking over each other, laughing to keep from crying while occasionally someone would pick a piece of grass out of my hair.

I snuck in the house to go into the living room and clean up any of the remnants of my rage, but it had been taken care of long ago. Mom came in, walking behind me, and rubbed my back.

"You're lucky I didn't like that coaster," she said before moving into the kitchen. That was the only comment on the fight earlier; for my thanks and blessings it was now forgotten.

While the sun went down we filled the house with joy. It kept surprising me how such a sad event could lead to so many happy stories.

Same as before my father was always felt, always missed, but it didn't stop us from laughing over the multiple rambles down memory lane.

Halfway through dinner, Llew got a phone call and came back fifteen minutes later to say that his girlfriend Cat was flying in tomorrow. She would be able to make it to the visitation and the funeral that way. He and I exchanged a smile. I was proud of Medi, who seemed truly happy. I'm sure she looked forward to meeting the woman who was special enough to come to such an event, but at the same time I'm sure it was driving her crazy that Llew seemed to be moving so fast. Just wait until she hears the news, I thought, smiling into my glass of wine.

After dinner we broke into little groups, Mom, Medi and I found ourselves doing the dishes and putting all the plates away. Everyone else seemed to be in the front room going through Dad's records and playing some of his favorites. The chore was restful, in the way certain things were, where your hands did the work and your brain could rest. The music filled the house and we didn't need to speak. The water was warm, the soap sudsy and I found myself thinking about sleep. Yet before I committed, the backdoor opened and Llew popped his head in.

"Lynman, your attendance is required outside."

I shook my head but didn't fight it. After drying my hands I followed him, glad to have an excuse to smoke. Outside, next to the trash cans were Llew and Brynn, smiling deviously.

"What's up?" I asked cautiously.

"You need a little comfort?" Llew said and winked, holding out a lit joint.

"Oh, come on you too, this is not going to happen. I've been drinking."

"Lynny Lynny Lynman, this is the perfect time to get a little bit trashed. I mean you've got me and Brynny to hold your hand. You're home, you're comfortable, and the viewing isn't until tomorrow night so you can sleep your concerns away."

"Peer pressure," Brynn whispered, and took a long drag.

"These are the days, you'll be happy you sailed through, oh so smoothly. These are the days, you'll look back and tell your grandkids about. Just make sure you write yourself a note," he said with a diabolical laugh.

I made sure not to look at my oblivious cousin when I pinched Llew and his big mouth.

Brynn danced a few steps. "Your evil cousin and your evil brother. There is no chance for escape, no one to blame but the two of us."

"If we smoke that, you know I'm just going to pass out. Is that what you want?" I asked hoping they didn't, but at the same time feeling my resolve begin to falter. They were both too good at talking me into it, and they had done it before, plus in truth part of me wanted to. It had been a really rough couple days. The idea of blanking for a night, sleeping the evening away, caught up in their jet stream, seemed pretty good.

Like my two favorite demons, I gave in and took the joint. Llew and Brynn high-fived while I took a deep draw of pot, way stronger than I realized. Yet, heck, I was ready to take a load off.

19

WEDNESDAY, BUT NOT YET WEDNESDAY

I woke up face planted into a plaid flannel sheet I had never seen before. It was full of Autumn colors of brown and orange. My head ached, feeling heavy and full of fog. I turned onto my back with a groan. It was like I had been hit by a truck, or slept in a concrete mixer. My neck was rigid, and it wasn't because I had slept wrong, but because I had slept afraid. I racked my brain to remember the last night. I tried and I tried, but it was completely lost. Where the fuck was Llew? Where the fuck was I? My body was telling me we had watched a horror movie, but that seemed ridiculous, why would we have done that I wondered. For all I knew, we had lived through a scary film. The last thing I remembered was us walking through the cemetery, laughing as the high overtook me.

"Fuuuuuuuuck," I mumbled under my breath, vowing that this sort of thing couldn't happen again and really believing it this time. I didn't like this feeling and it was time for this type of ridiculous situation to stop. I needed to be unmoving, a stone, or maybe a big oak tree. It didn't matter if Llew was beside me, or over at Brynn's place. No it didn't matter one bit. Being somewhere strange was not my idea of rest and relaxation. Family or not this was stupid. I sat up and saw I was fully dressed which was at least something to feel relief over. My shoes and my socks were gone. In my pocket was my phone. There was 5% battery life, which was better than nothing, I climbed to my feet and called Llew.

While the phone rang I looked around the room. It was pretty easy to recognize it was a man's room. There were heavy boots laid over next to the door, cologne on the bureau, and drawers that weren't pushed entirely in. The room wasn't dirty, but it wasn't overly clean. I glanced out the window and in a real *The Twilight Zone* type feeling I realized I was looking at my house.

"What the fuck Lynman? Do you know what time it is?" Llew whined.

"No, asshole, I don't know what time it is, but here is a question for you, where the fuck am I? What the fuck happened last night?" I whispered angrily through clenched teeth. It took longer than I wished, but I was finally realizing, this was Henry's house. I was in Henry's house, and in that moment of our relationship, it was exactly the opposite of where I wanted to be.

"Are you alright?" Llew asked. I could tell he was taking it seriously, my tone of voice wasn't the type of thing he could laugh at. I searched out his window across the way and saw him in the second floor room looking in my direction. We made eye contact from afar, and I both saw him laugh and heard it through the phone. I shook my head, not finding it funny.

"I can't be here Llew. I shouldn't have come here last night. I mean, what the fuck happened?"

"We went to a movie, we sort of just walked in. It didn't seem to matter what they were showing, but it was this really gory torture porn type thing, really shitty. I mean I thought it was funny, bad acting you know, but you just sort of freaked out. You made this weird noise like a dying animal, and just started sobbing. Brynn and I rushed you out the door. Luckily only like five people were there, but I couldn't bring you back to the house like that. Mom deals with a lot of our shit, but I wasn't about to pretend this was normal. We saw Henry in the cemetery and he offered to let you stay there. Nothing happened. Wait, tell me nothing happened?"

"Nothing happened, but I just can't see Henry right now, okay. Please, can you help me get out of here, quick."

"Why can't you see Henry?"

I sighed deeply and wanted to sit down, but more than that I wanted to sit down in my own bedroom, in my own home. "Don't make me say it Llew."

To my brother's great kindness he didn't push me. "See if you can open the window. I'll be right there."

I made one more glance around for my shoes or my socks and wondered hard if I could leave without them, but that really wasn't a question. I could and I would. The window after a moment's confusion with the latches, opened and the screen followed suit. I looked out the window. Below there was a wood pile that would make me about three very awkward feet closer to the ground, but being on the second floor the drop was still much more than I wanted. It was probably a good fourteen feet, meaning even if I hung from the window I would still fall far, too far. I didn't know if I was strong enough to hang. While I thought it over, I saw the front door open and Llew running across the yard and over toward me.

Shoeless and shirtless he was still smiling his crazy Llew smile and it helped a little bit. When he was beneath the window he just looked at me and shrugged.

"I could get a ladder?" he whispered.

"No, don't do that. It'll take too long."

"Well can you jump to the tree?" he asked.

Though one of the tree's limbs was almost in reach, the thin branch wouldn't hold me for more than a second. I just shook my head. Llew started to laugh.

"Shut up," I hissed, but I could almost laugh myself.

"Okay, jump."

"Jump?" I said thinking I had heard him wrong.

"Yeah, I'll catch you."

At that minute I heard a sound in the house. I'm not sure what it was, just a creak, but it was a creak that told me I wasn't alone, and so with little thought in the matter I sat in the window and swung one leg over.

"Just try not to kick me in the face," he said.

"You're not going to catch me. This is getting back at me for the laundry basket thing isn't it?"

I started to turn slightly and try to lower myself, my feet were doing everything they could to keep me clinging to the siding, as if I was climbing up instead of climbing down.

"You won't know until you try. Now, oh shit-" he said and smashed up against the wood pile ducking down.

I looked all around, not knowing what he saw, but I heard it.

"Llewellyn, what are you up to?" my mom called from across the street. She was in the driveway, still dressed in her robe and slippers and coming closer to get a better look.

"Nothing ma," he shouted, much too loud.

I saw him climb out of his hiding place and try to coax her back with hand signals but she didn't seem to notice. He was also glancing back at me while he did so, because I was starting to lose the strength that was keeping me securely on the wall. Mom moved closer and I began to drop significantly. Llew, not able to watch any longer, scrambled on top of the wood pile and took hold of my legs, trying to secure me, but as things were going from bad to worse he lost his footing at the same time that I started to release myself into him. All at once we fell, both of us scattering the wood in one loud clatter and whoop.

Llew started laughing as soon as he got his breath. "As graceful as ever," he said and slapped me hard on the ass.

My mother, whose hands were over her mouth, slowly lowered them and shook her head. She turned around without a word and walked back up the driveway. I looked up to the window from where I took the tumble and my stomach dropped further than I ever fell, glancing up I saw Henry looking out the window and down to where we lay. Our eyes locked in the moment. I thought he might make a joke or smile that mischievous smile he sometimes gave, but in a very unusual way his eyebrows dropped as if disappointed or hurt. He shook his head and closed the window.

"Dammit," I whispered, collapsing back, wishing I was anywhere else.

I looked back over at Llew and he smiled kindly before singing, "You're in love with Henry, you're in love with Henry."

"Oh, bite me." I said groaning, then climbed to my feet, pulling Llew after me.

We stacked the wood back where it was originally. Llew and I didn't talk while we did so. It was only after it was finished, and we both stretched our aches that I asked, "Do you know where my shoes are?"

"At home, you tossed them off while you were crying in the cemetery."

"I bet you're happy you talked me into smoking."

"It's the booze, maybe we just need to get you the right strain, or try some edibles?" he said unfazed.

"I could just not smoke," I said.

"You stop smoking cigarettes, and I'll stop trying to get you to smoke pot," he bargained.

I laughed without answering, thinking maybe this was a good enough reason to at least try.

20

MAKES US STRONGER

It was still early enough that the house was relatively quiet. We went in the front door and though I was sure I could have found Mom in the kitchen, and probably Milo too if I knew him; I just wasn't ready for people yet. I followed Llew up the stairs. He turned into the room where he was sleeping and I went to mine. I showed up at the right time. I could hear the shower and noticed Abe was missing, but still the bed wasn't empty. Brynn seemed to have taken advantage of my absence and was sleeping in my place. I pulled off my jeans and slipped on my shorts, unhooking my bra and pulling it free beneath my t-shirt. I crossed around the bed and fell into Abe's spot. I was asleep before I heard the shower turn off.

I'm not sure how long I was asleep, I fell into something deep and exhausted. When I finally woke up you could tell a bunch of time had passed. Everything still ached, the muscle memory of the horror film punishing me for bad choices. It was afternoon from the look of the sun through the window, and though the room was quiet and peaceful with the door closed, I could hear all the voices vibrating below. I took a quick shower. Tonight would be the viewing. I had some time, but I wasn't sure what else was going on that day that might need my attention.

I walked softly through the house, still yawning and starting to realize the most important thing to ensure my survival throughout the day would be a cup of coffee. Pushing through the swinging kitchen door, I walked in on Abe and Fletcher sharing a kiss. They pulled apart when I appeared. I was glad to see them both smiling, looking content to have each other so near.

Fletcher turned his light on me and I was nearly stopped in my tracks for a second. My brother-in-law is overwhelmingly handsome. He's Danish and about 6 foot 4, which helps add to the problem of his blond hair and blue eyes. The man is pretty much just a model, viking, esquire. He's over fifty now, but in the same way that Brad Pitt is over fifty; as in it doesn't matter. Early on in their relationship, every time he left we spent a few minutes catching each other's eye and wondering how Abe got someone so hot. I mean my brother is a handsome guy, but Fletcher, fuck. They've been together about fifteen years by now, luckily his magic only lasts for a few minutes before we all remember the weird things about him, like his dramatic sneezes and how he eats pizza with a fork. It's not too long until we're all able to be normal around him.

"Sleeping beauty," said Fletcher.

Heading towards the coffee I waved silently, before moving my hand over my mouth to hide a yawn. That's the position I was in when Fletcher swooped in and hugged me tightly. I took hold of the collar of his jacket with my pinned hand and wrapped my free arm around him.

"That's where you were going right?"

"Sorry, I got lost, of course," I said and hugged him back.

"Sorry, about your dad," he whispered, and I felt my shoulders go slack for a moment, as I remembered the weight I was carrying and all of the background baggage the news brought too. It hit me with a quick bit of *does Fletch know?* I hugged him tight.

"I might be becoming a hugging person after this week. Now, if you want me to stay a hugging person I'm going to need you to move aside from the coffee pot."

"Long night?" he asked while stepping out of the way.

"Exceedingly and it's only going to get better, right." I said while grabbing a mug and filling it up to the brim.

"Well you know what they say," he said, gearing up for a classic Fletcher pep talk. I always heard that if English wasn't your first language, you hated the random sayings that might not always make sense in a new language, but Fletcher seemed to cherish them, and to the family's annoyance Abe seemed to have picked up thrusting them into any given moment as well. "What doesn't kill you…"

"Um . . . makes you older? No, no, no, that's not it, makes you grayer?"

Fletcher sighed before walking past me and over to where Abe was leaning over the kitchen table reading something he had been writing. On his way past he poked me hard in the stomach.

"Ouch," I moaned. "Abe control your husband, tell him to keep his hands to himself."

Abe ignored us, Fletcher only winked, turning up his heat just enough that I got warm and forgot that I was annoyed at him. He leaned in over my brother, putting a hand on his neck and looking at what he was writing as well.

The door behind me opened and Llew came in carrying his own notebook. He poked me in the stomach in the same spot and I glanced down to see if there was a target. He checked the coffee pot and saw that it was one cup away from being empty. He knew by the family rule he would be forced to make a new pot, and so changed direction toward my cup. He slipped one arm around my shoulders and took the mug so he could take a sip.

"Abraham," he said, "read me what you're writing so I can speak first and steal it."

"I can't hear you," Abe said, not looking up.

"What are you guys doing?" I asked curiously, thinking it might be some sort of game.

"Writing something to read at the funeral about Dad. Medi is singing a song. I think Uncle A is reading a poem. When you're crying tomorrow I want it to be because of what I say, no other reason," said Llew. "What are you going to say?"

"I wasn't planning on saying anything," I said truthfully, having not even considered it before.

"You can't do that," Llew kept on, "we're his kids, it's expected."

I sort of just shook my head. "Says who?"

Llew flashed me a questioning look, and I quickly kept on. "Who says it's expected?"

"You might regret it down the way if you don't," Fletcher adds.

"I don't get it," Llew pushed, "you got so bent out of shape about the obituary. Now is your chance to put it right."

"The people at the funeral will all know who dad is, you don't go to a stranger's funeral. Sorry, but I have no desire to fucking perform."

"You're hungover kid, nothing's going to sound like a good idea right now," Fletcher said.

"Well you know what they say, if it doesn't kill you, you're just hungover." I felt really witty, but Fletcher frowned and I in turn felt bad. This wasn't what I wanted. "Sorry, Fletch, you're right. I'll be nicer after the coffee."

I carried the mug toward the back steps, but reached out and grabbed his hand on the way. He gave it a squeeze so I knew he wouldn't hold it against me.

Out on the back steps I was mad at myself, for being so angry. Fletcher was probably right, I just needed some time, but time wasn't my friend. Every day it seemed like I was making things worse, and I didn't know how to stop it. None of the choices I was making seemed bad in the moment, but here we were. Well, here I was, sitting on the back steps, drinking black coffee, feeling too many emotions for comfort. I pulled out a cigarette, adding more nails to my own figurative coffin.

I was taking a few poisoned breaths, when the door exploded back, swinging violently from the hinges and Llew was there.

"Come on, let's go."

"Go where?" I asked, thinking I must have missed something.

"I've got Mom's keys, and there is a plane we need to meet."

"Oh Llew, I'm really moving slowly today," I said.

"Cat's coming, we have to meet her plane."

"Okay, well, let me go grab my shoes."

"Why can't you keep an eye on your shoes. No time, and besides, when's the last time you flew? No shoes at the airport," he said so seriously I looked at his own feet and noticed he was at least wearing sandals. "Come on, we won't go in. We'll just pick her up at arrivals. Let's move it Lynman."

"Fine, fine," I grumbled.

We walked down to the car, me walking gently as the gravel made my feet ache. Llew reached over and grabbed the coffee and trotted down to the car sitting it on the hood, next he ran back and hunkered down in front so I would hop on for a piggy back ride of only about ten feet. He dumped me at the car door and carried the coffee back to his door, stealing another sip along the way.

"You know it really hurts my feelings that you'll go to the airport to get Cat, but wouldn't go to get me," he said earnestly.

"If I wasn't so in love with this coffee I would probably throw it at you."

"First it's the coaster, next it's a mug. You've got a nice little collection there."

With great annoyance I quoted one of our favorite movies, "Aunt Barbara, I love you but you're going to get it."

Llew laughed and clearing his throat he started to sing a tremendously horrible version of "Blue Velvet" as we backed down the drive.

21

NAVIGATING

We drove along the turnpike to the airport. I really love being on long drives. It's hard not to fall asleep though if I'm tired. Thankfully that's not how I was feeling at that moment. My sleep schedule and my emotions were all fucked up but strangely enough in that moment I was just so overwhelmingly relaxed. It had a lot to do with being there next to my brother far from the issues at home, in a situation that was always just so comfortable. Llew and I spent a couple years doing a lot of driving around. I never wanted to learn to drive, it was like pulling teeth to make me get my license, but not Llew. From the moment he was old enough for his permit it was all he wanted. For months he nagged, tricked, bribed and begged every legal adult to take him out and once he had his license I became his navigator. So much of our pocket money turned into gas money. We would just disappear on day trips every couple weeks, from breakfast to dinner just exploring the countryside.

It was our thing, and we never really told people about where we went. We cruised through Amish country, and found high hills to act as our roller coasters that dropped low while our hands were held up high. We drove all over New York City, all the boroughs, getting lost in a quagmire of stress and loud horns searching for the argumentative best pizza slice. Even though Llew had a string of girlfriends throughout high school and he was busy on and off, we would always make time for these drives. The worst punishment's Mom and Dad could meet out was to take away his car keys. And even when that happened we might sneak out at night with the extra key and silently push the car down the driveway. I got good at pushing the rusty gray green Toyota Tercel all those years.

I was thinking about all of this while Llew switched lanes, messed with Mom's radio, and looked so at ease. God, he annoyed me. God, he was my best friend.

"Hey," he shouted, "do you remember that time Dad went to get the oil changed and he realized I had put about five thousand miles on the car in three months, and we kept trying to get him to believe someone must have broken in and changed the odometer."

"Yeah, I'm pretty sure we missed the winter carnival because of that. We weren't very good liars. I don't know how he put up with us."

"Yeah, he was a special man," Llew wiped roughly at his eye and turned the music up. He found some old Journey song and we sang loudly at the top of our lungs.

Once the song was over, Llew seemed to have changed the direction of his brain and turned the music back down to say, "So, are you going to tell me about what's up with you and Henry?"

"Nope," I said flatly and tried to reach back for the radio knobs.

He knocked my hand away, "Come on, Lynman, you know you can trust me."

"Dude, you've got the big secret okay, just concentrate on keeping that."

"Come on," he whined.

"It's just so nice to know you were surprised."

"Well not really, you've always been in love with Henry, that was obvious. We just never thought you would act on it."

I could only grimace and look out the window.

"Do you think Medi knows?" I asked.

"Ha," he shouted, but didn't explain any more.

It didn't take long until we pulled up to the airport. It was a mess of cars and lanes and we circled about three times until Llew's phone blew up to say Cat was waiting at the third column or something.

I'm not sure who I expected, but it wasn't who was waiting, even with the pictures I'd seen. Cat was slight, she was small, well I suppose I'm about one inch taller, so I guess she wasn't so small. She seemed young, college-aged young, though she was twenty-five, with straight jet black hair and dark skin. The girl who waited with her roller bag looked shy and nervous until the minute she recognized Llew in the window and smiled with genuine happiness. We pulled over and I climbed out of the front seat, bare feet and all. Llew ran around the car and swept her up, giving her a Hollywood type kiss, before setting her back on the ground and not letting her go. He dropped down and placed one more kiss on her stomach before whispering something I couldn't hear. When he turned to look at me, I couldn't help but be truly happy myself. Jeez if he could stay that happy for the rest of his life, I knew I could probably die mediocre myself. It's amazing how much strength you can get from knowing the folks around you are content and safe.

"Cat," he said, "this is Emlyn. Lynman this is Ehecatl."

"Call me Cat," she said.

"It's Aztec," Llew whispered.

Cat rolled her eyes. "Actually it's Nahuatl, Llewellyn" she replied.

"Nahuatl," he repeated.

"Llewellyn," I echoed and Llew bared his teeth at me. "You can call me any number of things. Family calls me Lynman."

She and I just sort of smiled at each other silently for a second, before I said, "I'm glad you were able to come. I'm glad we can all meet you."

"I wish it could have been under better circumstances."

"Yeah, c'est la vie and jazz," I said with a shrug.

Cat and I shared a quick hug and then I forced her into the front seat, promising her I had strong plans to fall asleep in the next five minutes and this way she could get the grand tour.

I struck rather strongly to my claims and began to fade in and out for most of the drive back. The sun was warm on the window and it didn't seem to matter how much I had slept that morning, the trick of the car claimed me once again. I woke up once and saw we had stopped someplace I didn't recognize. The car was pulled over on the side of the road and there was some sort of tiny store with windows that read, BAIT, ALCOHOL, FIREWORKS, COFFEE, ROAD FOOD. I wasn't excited enough by the road food to fully wake back up and faded again before the two came back to the car.

At last we were driving through town, and I think there was something to those memorable turns that my body recognized even in sleep because I was up and blinking.

"She's awake," Llew shouted.

"I'm awake," I mumbled through a yawn. "I hope these views are all that you've dreamt of Cat?"

"Fall is my favorite time of year, you just don't get this back home. My parents actually don't live too overly far from here. They moved to a suburb outside of Philadelphia last year. My older sister had twins."

"Word on the street is that twins run in families," I said, shaking off the last of the sleep, feeling truly great, the hangover gone, the car nap certainly refreshing.

"You shut your mouth Lynman," Llew said as if I might say two babies into being.

"If you'll forgive me for saying Cat, I just want to point out to my brother that you have a nice-sized head."

Llew laughed so loud and hard that he pulled over to the side of the road to get himself back under control. Cat only shook her head, before saying "Thanks, I think. You two are just what I imagined."

"Thanks, I think," Llew and I responded nearly in unison, tripping over each other's words.

We pulled into the driveway and same as with Uncle Amos and Brynn, people started spilling out of the house. I think they were glad for different things to concentrate on. Cat was brave to come into this mess. She was manhandled with hug after hug from pretty much everyone. Finally, we wandered back into the house in twos and threes. The afternoon flew by, people started getting changed for the viewing. It was hard to find a room or a bathroom that was empty and available for changing into formal mourning clothes.

I let myself wait until the last minute, enjoying all the rush around me moving from one conversation to the next. I was just glad to be in a more social mood for my family. I didn't budge until Mom appeared looking beautiful, fixing her earrings and said, "You better get a move on Lyn, thirty minutes."

I shooed Abe and Fletcher out of my room, which had become theirs for the rest of the time that they were at the house, but I still needed it to get changed. My new dress hung on the wall and once it was on I breathed a sigh of relief that it still looked the way I remembered from the mall. I sat down at the desk to slip on my shoes, but before I did that I had to move the laundry basket which I first noticed Sunday night. I knew Dad had set it there, ever since I first noticed it. It could have been Mom of course, but Dad was the one free that day, the one who liked to fold the clothing just so. I was proved right by the sight of the socks, laid perfectly on top of each other and folded in half, with just enough of a tuck at the top to make sure they stayed mates.

It wasn't just folded clothes in the basket, but the letter from UCLA. I sighed to see it. I would put it away for now. I didn't want to think about college or California for a while. I grabbed the heavy envelope and realized there was something written there. Dad's smooth neat miniscule cursive filled the blank side.

Hon, I read and stopped myself suddenly. I didn't know what this was, but I knew what it really was. It was the last thing my dad left for me. I felt my eyes welling up, and hopped to my feet as if it was a dangerous situation. I couldn't read this now. I laid it on the desk and stepped away as if it was corrosive to touch, but before I got to the door I stopped again just thinking about it.

"Lynman, move your ass," Llew shouted.

"Llewelyn, was that really necessary," Fletcher said, his voice carrying upstairs. He must have been standing right next to Llew when he shouted.

I knew that they were waiting for me. I needed to leave, but there was a tug much stronger back to the desk. I turned back and grabbed the envelope. I started to read.

Hon, there is so much to explain. So much for us to talk about. I'm just trying to get my thoughts down. It might be easier for you to read this than to hear it. I hated seeing you leave like that. Knowing you were hurt. Your mother and I just got off the phone with Abe, I told them that the jig was up, the broth spoiled. We had waited too long. It would have been better to have talked this over before and that's on me. When you're ready to talk we're here for-

A hand touched my shoulder and I jumped, turning sideways, and seeing Abe there.

"Didn't you hear me?" he said. "I was calling your name." His voice trailed off. It must have been something in my eyes. He reached for the envelope. I think he saw Dad's handwriting. It meant so much now. It was worth more than money, these little pieces of him and he narrowed in on it. I'm not sure how much he read, before I cut him off.

"You know?"

He rubbed his palm up his cheek and nodded while doing so. "Of course I know."

"But you know, that I know. I mean you knew this whole time?"

Abe opened his mouth, but he was cut off, Brynn ran up the stairs.

"C'mon, c'mon, c'mon. The train is leaving, pulling out of the station," she said while pulling an invisible horn.

Not glancing back Abe said, "Brynn, you all go ahead, we'll be right behind you."

She looked at us suspiciously but started to slide out of the room.

"Actually, we should go," I said quickly, not meeting Abe's eyes.

"Lynny, we need to talk."

"We can't talk now. Okay, not now. Not before seeing all these people."

He seemed like he might disagree with me, but in the end he nodded his head. I wanted to say something, but I couldn't. I ran down the stairs on Brynn's heels.

"I'm quoting your mother, 'It's about time,'" Fletcher said before groaning, "we're still one short. Where's Abe?"

"I'm right here," he called down, looking a shade paler than was normal, but forcing a smile. Fletcher caught his hand noticing the change, but I hurried on leaving them behind.

We jetted outside, and I jumped into the car with Milo, Bennie and my sister.

"You look nice," said Milo.

"What? I mean thanks. You all too."

"It's a good dress." said Medi.

"Thanks, for helping me find it," I said, trying to focus. I reached up and touched her arm.

"Of course, that's what sisters are for."

22

FIREWORKS

The viewing was probably the best place for me. Everywhere people looked grief stricken and held private conversations with forced smiles. It was strange, hours of people coming and going, sometimes quiet, sometimes loud. My father wasn't there. He had decided to be cremated, yet halfway through the viewing I realized he was actually there; his remains were in the urn. I had to sit down after realizing that. A large heavy wooden box engraved with a willow tree sat on a long table surrounded by pictures, trophies, a baseball, and a dusty copy of Robin Hood, with his name written inside the cover in childish scrawl. During those hours, I was trying to not become overwhelmed. I know my face showed the battle brewing within me, but it was easy to hide, because people expected it. Time flew by, and before I knew it we were home, searching for a second wind.

I did what I could to stay busy once we were back. I changed quickly out of my nice clothes, and drank, avoiding Abe as much as I could. Part of me needed to go back and read the rest of my dad's note but I couldn't, same as I couldn't have the conversation with Abe. All that time he and my mom knew about Sunday. It was hard to know how I felt. To rebuild the last few days under a different gaze. I think more than anything I was embarrassed. There was no secret. There were only lies. Lies we all shared.

I snuck the letter out of my room while I was changing. *Hon*, I saw the word once again and shoved it in my pillowcase with a few things, like my pajamas, because I knew I would probably end up sleeping someplace random, like a couch or a floor. I hid it in a downstairs closet and tried not to think about all the information waiting on me.

We warmed up some of the casseroles that had been dropped off. Tomorrow after the funeral there would be a lot of people coming over, a whole spread of food was planned, so Mom wanted to make sure we subtracted from the refrigerator, didn't add. We drank, and we ate. The house was so full. Part of my life everywhere.

Cat seemed to be holding up well, but I think my family was on their best behavior. I sat down next to her at one time as she watched Llew and Brynn play the game where they tried to slap each other's hands before they were pulled away. Brynn was fast but she had to be. A slap from Llew left a mark.

"Be careful," I heard Cat say, as Brynn shook her hand painfully.

"May I ask you something?" I said.

"Of course," she turned to face me. I think she was happy to look away from their game.

"Is this the Llew you know, or do we bring the worst out of him?"

Cat laughed. "I wouldn't say the worst, but he does seem a bit more rambunctious. More at ease, but happier. I can see how comfortable you all are with each other. It seems like a lovely family."

"Yeah, it's pretty great," I said truthfully but suspicious of my own words.

Llew seemed to get even more comfortable, because it took me by surprise when all of a sudden. I was pulled away from a chat with Amos, by the sound of him clearing his throat. He shouted to get everyone's attention.

"Hey everyone, is this everyone? Bennie, are you back from the shitter? Where are you Lynman?"

"Present," I called.

"So, I've decided since I have you all here. It might be the right time to say something. I've been debating whether to bring it up. I mean we all know why we're here. We're here for Dad," he nodded his head and pulled Cat into him tightly trying to shore himself up. "The thing about family is, well, we don't just lose people, we gain people."

"Oh my god, are you two engaged?" Medi said with a smiling bit of shock. Looking all around the room for people to catch an eye with.

"Oh Lord no," Llew said and I couldn't help but laugh sharply.

"What I am, is a father. Well, I suppose father to be, but since my tadpole is in there swimming, I guess I'm a dad now."

All around the room, people shouted. My mother, who had been looking nervous through it all, started to cry and pulled Cat into her arms. Medi still looked shocked. She looked at me and I shrugged before smiling back. It was a truly joyous moment though with the bittersweet aftertaste that my father was missing out.

"You're going to have to call that baby Lycurgus if it's a boy," Fletcher said smiling.

"You should name her Lycurgus if she's a girl," I added.

"Oh god, who would do that to a child," said Cat with enough of a straight face to make me laugh, "well, maybe a middle name. We can discuss it."

Who would do that to a child? Hearing her say Dad's words it felt like maybe he was there after all, maybe just a little bit.

Brynn started passing around drinks to celebrate and we all drank a bit more. Mom, practically glowing, finally pulled herself away because it was getting late and tomorrow would be long with an early start. Cat went with her. We seemed to forget the fact that this poor pregnant woman had traveled from a different coast and might not be up for a late night party with the rest of us.

People kept yawning. I felt tired myself and was trying to think of a place to crash. My sleep schedule was destroyed and I was hoping to make up for some of the strange bits of sleep that the last few days had been anchored around, but Llew was still wired and I watched a thought come to his mind.

"Oh shit," I heard him say. "Newman siblings, mount up. I'm talking to you too, Newman-Washington. We have work to do."

"I think my work is in bed," I said.

"Soon, little sister, soon. Medi, Abe, you ready?"

"Ready for what?" Abe asked cautiously.

"Okay," Medi said, a little bit more drunk than she usually gets and struggling out of the comfy chair.

Llew grabbed Abe's hand and started pulling him out the door. Medi grabbed my arm and we trailed after.

Outside, Llew ran to Mom's car and popped the trunk, from there he pulled out a paper bag. While he was messing with it, I heard Medi shout, "Oh, Henry."

Automatically Llew, Abe and I smiled and repeated her words at a whisper as we had many times before. *O Henry,* we would say before making up a statement about candy or writing.

Henry waved at Medi and smiled. She ran over and hugged him.

"Henry, are you in?" Llew asked without explanation.

"I'm thinking, no," he said looking at the state of us. I was doing everything I could to look at him without actually looking at him.

"You're in," Medi said. "You're an official or maybe it's unofficial Newman. I'm a little drunk."

"What are you doing?" he asked.

"We have no idea," Abe said and tried to get a look inside the mysterious bag.

"Run for your life," I muttered.

"Shush, you won't know until it's time for you to know. Lynman, lead the way," said Llew.

I wasn't sure where I was going, but he was gesturing toward the cemetery, so I started walking. Llew bumped me with his hip and I quickened my step to keep up with his long strides. It didn't take too long to figure out where we were heading. The cemetery was dark, it was closed. At least it was meant to be closed at dusk, but as we got deeper in we began to hear sounds from the playground.

"Don't these kids have school?" I found myself hiccupping, annoyed, "I mean it's my bedtime. It should at least be theirs."

"You are so old," Llew said painfully.

"I don't know what you've planned," I said with wild gestures, "but I do not trust it. Remember what we have here, are children."

"I can't believe my baby brother is going to have a baby," Medi said to Henry.

"Llew, you're having a kid?" asked Henry. "Congrats, brother."

"Thanks, we're excited, not exactly planned, but-"

"Well, that sounds like our Llewellyn to a T. You are going to have to grow up, time to start being an adult," Medi said, shaking her head.

"Last time I checked, I was an adult," snapped Llew.

Medi laughed. "You have no idea what you're getting into. Oh, but you're going to find out. This isn't like a dog you can just give away on Craigslist."

"Actually, I think you can drop babies off at the fire station," I said, trying to interrupt the argument it seemed Llew and Medi were brewing towards.

"All I'm saying," Medi said, "is you're not known for making the best choices. Don't just ask me, Abe?" she beckoned.

My oldest brother sort of waved it off, but at the last minute gestured ambiguously towards Llew. "She has a point. It'll be hard."

"Of course it will be hard," I snapped. "Raising children is hard. Llew fucking knows that."

Llew opened his mouth, but shut it. I could see his gears turning, his desire to say something backhanded. The comebacks were there, but he knew he had promised to keep my secret, even though his secret was out. He didn't know that my secret was out as well, and I couldn't let that moment pass for Llew, and so instead I said it. "Too bad Dad won't be around, if he was you could always give your kid to him and Mom to raise."

"Don't-" Medi started to talk but stopped as she took in what she had heard. She looked at all three of us, and then leaned heavily on Henry's shoulder. "Yeah, I definitely drank too much."

"Ha," Llew laughed a hard laugh. He had forgotten his frustration with Medi at that moment.

"Emlyn you don't understand everything," said Abe.

"That's funny, because I would say I don't understand anything, not a fucking thing."

"So is this when we're doing this? Drunk and in the middle of the cemetery?" Abe said stiff and determined to stand his ground if given the chance to talk.

Drunk and in the middle of the cemetery seemed like the exact place to do this. "I'm just sick of all these lies. Everything we say to each other are lies. I mean adopted. I thought I was adopted most of my life. Do you have any idea how that feels?"

"I'm sorry," Abe said.

"I just want the truth. I don't-"

"Bullshit," said a voice interrupting me. I looked back and saw Henry. I had practically forgotten he was there. I didn't know what he was saying, I opened my mouth with a question, but he cut me off.

"You have a real one-sided view on the truth, Em. I'm sorry, I know that the things you are dealing with right now are big, enormous, but I want you to think it over. Stop playing dumb for a few minutes. Take a look in the mirror and think about this honesty you hold so dear."

Henry unfolded Medi from his arm and turned back down the hill toward his house.

"I'm so confused," my sister mumbled.

Llew put up his hand as if asking permission and I shrugged.

"You see Medi-usa dear, Lynman just found out that Abraham is her birth father, and our same Lynman loves O Henry."

"Oh Henry," she repeated. Medi just looked at the three of us, her eyes started to close. She swayed, a little wobbly on her feet and finally said, "Tell me again tomorrow, okay?"

The four of us stood there, no one knowing what more to say, or what to do. My anger was checked by Henry. He had me wracking my brain a bit. The alcohol didn't help. I looked over at Llew, and he just shrugged. I shrugged back and I guess the movement was enough to invite him to keep on with the original plan.

Llew opened up the bag and started passing out the items inside. I realized it was fireworks. It immediately clicked back to the stop on the way back from the airport. He gave us all roman candles as well as smaller fireworks. We walked without speaking, getting closer to the playground, hunkered down. My brain was spinning, but I was glad to have the fireworks to focus on to keep me going. Finally, Llew, who had been leading the charge, made a fist, holding up his hand to check us.

"Lighter," he whispered, and I pulled mine out. He had his as well. He lit one of the small crackers. It was a smoke bomb, he violently urged me to light more. Somewhere in the mix there was a stink bomb too. We tossed them all towards the playground and the dark plume of smoke surrounded the kids swinging beneath the park lamps. It blocked out the lights, and seemed to enhance the sound as we heard gasps, shouting, and cussing. The shake of metal chains as the swings were abandoned. Next, Llew started lighting the roman candles we all held. They shot fiery balls of flame through the darkness. The kids screamed and ran. Medi screamed as well and I started to laugh. My chest hurt, I was laughing so hard. I looked over and Abe was smiling.

"Get gone," Llew shouted like the adult he was. "This here is Newman land."

We took the hill, running up it into the mix of smoke and smell. I ran up after Llew, pulling my shirt past my nose and fell into the rubber seat of the playground equipment. I was still laughing as I started to swing. Laughing and coughing on the smoke and stink I pumped my legs back and forth. Medi and Abe joined us. There were enough swings and in the dark I heard the chains and I heard feet drag in gravel and all the anger was gone. All the worry and shame that was so rampant hardly five minutes before was shoved aside for that moment. I knew nothing was forgotten. We still had a full day ahead, and conversations that might hurt feelings, but swinging in the dark with the smell of rotten eggs seeping into my clothing, I was happy. I was happy with my family.

23

THURSDAY, BUT NOT YET THURSDAY

I slept on the old couch in the garage. It was cold and I was buried in blankets. I'm sure there was space in one of the rooms, but I greatly appreciated the lack of snoring. Even so, I hardly slept, my brain was just trying to deal with everything. I was surprised that I wasn't forced to continue dealing with the angry half-truths of that night. Around the same time the smoke was fading from the fireworks, we went home. We did so pretty quietly. Abe stood up and we followed him, walking stretched out, lingering, but staying on the path so we didn't trip over the headstones. When we neared Henry's house my eyes went up to one of the windows in the back. The light was on and I thought I saw a shadow. The shadow followed me home and so now lying in bed it was not the business between Abe and I, which I played over, but the mess with Henry.

He had called me out for doing the same thing that had bugged me. Hypocrite, what an ugly word. It seemed like everyone knew I had feelings for him, even Henry. There was no pretending it was something else. There was no ignoring it, and even though it was hard and difficult and there was a chance I was going to embarrass myself, well, continue to embarrass myself; I still had to talk to him. Whatever the conversation would be, it would shed light on the truth. Hidden behind the lies was the truth that I loved Henry, and like that I realized something. Lies or not I was loved, by my dad, by my mom, by Abe, by Medi and Llew. Hurt or not, I loved all of them.

I sat up finding perhaps the sober eye in that night's storm and turned on the light. Dad's work bench was there, and I found some drafting paper he would use, and an old carpenter's pencil, but before I wrote anything I took the UCLA stamped envelope that I had recovered earlier. It still showed that thoughtful cursive penmanship that I'd come to recognize on shopping lists and bills and notes of love to all of us. It was time to finish reading my dad's letter.

Hon, there is so much to explain. So much for us to talk about. I'm just trying to get my thoughts down. It might be easier for you to read this than to hear it. I hated seeing you leave like that. Knowing you were hurt. Your mother and I just got off the phone with Abe, I told them that the jig was up, the broth spoiled. We had waited too long. It would have been better to have talked this over before and that's on me. When you're ready to talk we're here for you.

When Abraham told us you were coming. It took us a bit by surprise. He was still figuring out who he was and a father by 16 was not something any of us expected. Even so, we never had any doubt that we wanted you, that you were a part of this family and we would love you and give you everything we could, as a parent or grandparent it didn't matter. We always planned to tell you the truth when you were older. When you and Abe were both older.

I blame myself, I was so staunch in my determination that you would know your father, but in the end it was me who couldn't let go of the lie and it was my heart that faltered, because you see, and this might be hard to understand; you Darling Emlyn called me Dad. I work amongst words, I know their power and I fell entirely within their trap.

That might not seem like so much, but between you and I, you come from a family of mother lovers. Three times in a row the first word my children uttered was mom. Abe seemed to cling to the word, with such emphasis, mama. When Medi came around she said mommy with those big, beautiful, loving, eyes, and then our Llewellyn. I swear all we heard was mamamamamama nonstop for days. You should have been no different, you were raised no differently, you slept in Abe's footy pajamas, you had Medi's elephant, you and Llew shared the same crib, but even so, the first word we ever heard you utter was Dada and you did so looking at me. You stole my heart and in turn I think I led the charge in putting us in today's pickle, because it was after hearing that word I became your father, and in turn I stole that from Abraham.

But let's move forward a few years. We should never have told you that you were adopted, that was another mistake. A quick lie, a bandage on the leaking ship. I think if you forgive us for the rest you may never forgive us for that one. The lies we told ourselves grew to match the one we pressed on you. I always told myself, it didn't matter if you knew the whole truth because we were your parents, it made no difference. The love we shared in this family was the only thing that mattered.

I'm sorry my girl, and not just for the hurt I've caused you. I look at Abraham and I see how he watches you. He watches you the same way I watch him. I will never say that I am not your father, I will take that title to the grave as my greatest pride, same as with Abe, Medi and Llewelyn. Yet know that there is still more for you. Recognize that Abe is not just your brother. It's not an easy secret he carried, a decision we as his parents guided him towards with little choice in the matter.

Recently, I've been speaking a lot with Abe about taking over the store, and he could use our help. I never said anything and maybe you can help me keep a secret, but I always hoped one of you kids would find a place there. To look at those walls and those books and see more than physical things, but stories, histories, imagination and a place we all grew up together. Your mom and I are still growing. I admit one of my greatest joys in life is being able to raise you kids at the store and see each of you in turn find your own love in reading.

Now when it comes to our Abe and our store. He could use a partner in that undertaking. If you really want to go to California and continue your search, then I wish you all the happiness, all the luck and all the suc-

cess that you can claim. But I want to tell you something else Emlyn and this is as a father to his daughter. The things you are searching for aren't tied to a location. You aren't going to find them in a place. You won't find them in a job. Maybe this is our fault. Maybe this lie you've been led to believe has created a hole in your heart that you search to fill, and if anything good comes from these hard conversations maybe that hole can begin to heal. Remember the puzzles we put together from the shop. It wasn't hard to figure out what the picture was, but we wouldn't be happy, we wouldn't be finished, not without all the pieces. I hope these answers are one such piece. Everything you search for you'll find in yourself. Though consider my dear girl, it was always easier to put the puzzles together with the helping hands of the people you love. Oh Emlyn, you're a blessing that gives off a light and I promise you'll get it back tenfold. You're good at it, I mean you've been fixing this old heart from your first word.

Love,
Your Father

I stared at the letter when I finished reading it. I read it through again. I looked at the word father. I looked at many of the words and then I started to write. I felt calmer, because of what I had read, stronger and I tried to pass that through the pencil. It took me a long time to get all the words right. When it was finally finished. I slapped the light switch off and fell back on the couch. This time I crashed. It wasn't too cold and my brain was quiet. It was a perfect place to rest.

HOME

Mom woke me up. "My goodness, we've been looking for you. Why in the world did you choose this place?"

"It was either this or the floor. Someone told me I couldn't sleep at the bookstore."

"Well, now you're going to need to hurry. You four all look a mess this morning and smell terrible. I hope you didn't get into too much trouble last night."

"No cops, but if they come by, we were all asleep by ten, okay?"

Mom shook her head, "Here take this." She passed me her mug of coffee.

"You're a queen," I said.

"No, just a mom," she answered and turned to leave.

"Mom," I said, stopping her, struggling with the words. "I just want to say, thanks."

She knew I wasn't thanking her for the coffee.

"Emlyn, there are things you never have to say thank you for, but if you are feeling generous I imagine you know when to make your feelings known."

"You just had your birthday."

"I was thinking about May," she said seriously.

"Mother's Day," I answered.

"Mother's Day," she repeated. "Now, move it."

***

The service and the funeral that followed were pretty quiet affairs. Medi cried, Abe made me cry and Llew made me laugh. I struggled with the idea of not talking in that moment, but it felt true and I had to be good with that decision. We managed to smile as all of us piled into the limo. It was a strange drive helping to lead the funeral train. Seeing those sad faces that we passed. It took us almost all the way home, back to the cemetery. A cemetery that we were all so attached to. A cemetery we treated like our back yard and here it was trying to tamper with that joy, but I wouldn't let it. I was happy to have Dad so close. To have him right where I needed him for all the years to come.

Once he was laid to rest, we walked back to the house. When we stopped by Mrs. Hayden's grave, I laid the flower down that I'd been handed by an usher. Mom smiled at me. "You know it's always meant the world to Henry, you taking the time to look after her. He's mentioned it more than once. He can see you from her sewing room. That poor boy, he could use someone in his life."

"Yeah, Mom I'm sure he could," I said and smiled, but hoped to change the conversation nonetheless.

"Life is too short and you're not getting any younger."

"Mother dear," I said in a less than loving tone.

She kissed my head and we walked home silently arm in arm.

I hadn't talked with Henry that morning. I only caught a couple glimpses of him from across the funeral home and then in the crowd at the cemetery. One time we locked eyes and I gave him a bit of a crooked smile, which he mirrored back, but looked away from soon after. I wasn't heartbroken by the response. Last night and these past few days didn't just disappear. I needed to talk to him.

Back at the house things were busy. It was shoulder to shoulder in a couple places. The biggest party we'd ever had, and it didn't make me as sad as I expected. Instead I found myself proud that it was for Dad. People I knew from all my life, people I never met but knew me. They just kept showing up, happy and sad. In one breath someone might be crying and then all of a sudden, the sadness was just shaken loose by a roar of joy that flooded in the telling of a story. I came up on Uncle Amos talking about the time we went camping and Dad pretended there were bears on the loose. Abe and Medi were adults by that trip and rolled their eyes while Llew and I looked exceedingly nervous. None of us knew that Dad had called Uncle Amos, who showed up about twenty minutes after we had all laughed it off. There we were, sitting around the campfire when the trees started shaking, roars rang through the woods, and the next minute Abe and Medi were locked in the car. We laughed over the story, and the next minute folks were wiping away tears, but not me. I remembered Dad holding me tight, saying the bear wouldn't get me as long as he was there. I believed him.

I didn't feel that weight of secrecy that day either. When Mom had mentioned Henry on our walk home, I knew that she knew I was in love with him. When Fletcher gave me a hug, there wasn't a wall of worry I carried. He knew the same things I knew, nothing changed, the news didn't matter. We were a family, and families lie to each other. They also forgive each other. There are loving lies and there's a real truth in that. It's something I hold as an almost cosmic belief.

After dinner the house started to empty. The street lamps turned on. The house was still full but it was the right number of people. Mom, Abe, Fletcher, Medi, Milo, Bennie, Llew, Cat, Uncle Amos and Brynn. We changed into comfy clothes, and filled plates with leftover food.

Brynn and I had a long chat, when we snuck out back to smoke by the trash cans, and I made her tell me the whole story of our Saturday night. After the telling, she seemed worried that she had caused all of this, it was a worry I recognized. I shook it off, glad to know the truth. When we finished I gave her a hug.

"Thank you," I whispered, "also I'm never getting high again. So don't even try me."

"Whatever you say cuz, maybe you'll be a good influence on me."

"I wouldn't go that far," I laughed.

Back inside everyone seemed exhausted.

"There is too much cleaning to do," Mom said looking at all the mess.

"We can always move, burn down the house, claim the insurance," I said.

"Don't worry," said Fletcher ignoring me, "we'll get it."

"Who's we?" I asked.

"I think we found our first volunteer," Uncle Amos applauded me, and I smiled. He changed direction and added, "by the way, I just want to say that was a beautiful song you sang, Medi. I was proud of all of you."

"I wish you had said something Lyn," Medi said. "Whatever you wanted to say, would have been alright."

I could tell some of the folks were nervous with Medi saying that, and I was curious how much she remembered from the night before. I only shrugged. "I understand wanting to say something, but I just didn't feel the need. He's my father. He knew I loved him. You're my family, you know I still love him. What else matters?"

Abe nodded.

"But also, I did write something, and I thought about reading it, but in the end, it was something I really only wanted to share with you all. So, if I can borrow a few moments." I cleared my throat dramatically, and made a show of taking the paper out of my pocket and shaking it open with a loud snap. I took a deep breath and looked at Llew waiting for him to make some sort of comment, but he just smiled.

"Lycurgus Mitchell Newman was born March 7, 1954 in New Carlisle, Maine. His father, Mitchell was a butcher, and his mother, Janet was a nurse. Lycurgus used to say it was the perfect family to be born into, to have a father who could cook and a mother who could keep them healthy. Growing up, Lycurgus couldn't decide whether he wanted to be a baseball player or a writer, but once he realized he wouldn't be able to throw a strike to Yogi Berra, the decision was made easy. In 1972, he enrolled in Dandridge College and studied Literature. It was there he met Amos Mills, a man of many gifts. The two were lifelong friends. Amos filled his head with stories, and helped fill his heart by the introduction of his sister, the artist, Susan Mills. He often said he didn't understand Susan's art, but the fact that he bought three pieces just for the excuse to see her, made him know it was true love. After a very brief courtship Lycurgus asked Susan to marry him. Together, the two raised four children. The eldest, Abraham Mills Newman known for making every unfortunate event fortunate and a man whose presence is a blessing. Second born, Medi Janet Newman Washington, whose ferocious love of her family is never put in question, and lives for them with as much passion as she lives for herself. Youngest son, Llew Sanford Newman, is still known as Baby Joy even though he is almost 30, and has been everyone's best friend since the day he was born. And the fourth born, Emlyn Susan Newman who continues searching and reaching always because her family never let her know there was a limit on her dreams.

"Their family is an extended one, Milo Washington the sturdiest tree in the forest, Bennie Washington, built of hope and sunlight, Brynn Mills who will always step first if you're dragging your feet, Fletcher Hopkins who crushes doubt and demands the best of us, and Ehecatl Lopez, brave enough to charge into the lion's den. Though Lycurgus goes before, he will never be gone, as he is survived by more than family, but by the example he set down, and the love that made us grow.

"Come visit the Fiction's Family Book Store, family run business since 1980, presently guided and guarded by Abraham and Emlyn Newman, bring in this obituary and receive 10% off your next purchase."

I sniffed loudly when I finished and wiped a tear away before saying, "That's actually a joke since it's not running in the paper."

Llew was smiling, "So you aren't leaving? You're going to stay and work the store?"

"I think so," I said, "as long as Abe will have me."

"Wait," Medi asked. "Abe are you moving home?"

Abe could only nod his head. He was crying and wiped his eyes before coming over to hug me. It was a good hug.

"Sorry, if I let the cat out of the bag?" I whispered.

"Not at all."

"I'm sorry," I said.

"You've got nothing to apologize for. I'm sorry."

"Fuck that, I'm happy." I took Dad's note out of my pocket and handed it to him. "He might have written this to me, but I think it's something you should read too. He's always been good with helping to put things in perspective. Even now."

Abe nodded, still wiping at tears.

I glanced at my other brother. "Sorry Llew, I might have jumped the gun with the California dreaming."

"Not at all, actually thank god," Llew said loudly. "I had no idea how I was going to tell you Lynman, but with the baby, and with Cat's family so close. You know there's no way we're going to stay in California much longer."

Everyone was either smiling or crying or cheering. I never felt so right, so at home. Well almost.

"As much as I'd like to stop everything and do those dishes right now, there's one more thing I've got to try and fix." I looked over at Fletcher, before saying. "I guess what doesn't kill us, makes us stronger. Now, if you might forgive me and give me a few minutes of your time, Abey Baby, Medi-My, Llewser. I have one more thing I need to borrow you three for."

THE TRUTH

Abe nodded, still wiping away tears, Llew jumped to his feet, and Medi cheered. They followed me to the garage where I had been taking up residence since last night. Once inside, I pulled Henry's striped sweater out of my pillowcase and put it on. The three of them watched silently, sharing curious glances as we headed outside and walked out into the street. The sun had gone down and it was dark. My heart dropped to see the lights off at Henry's house, but before I got too worried. I stopped and looked at Medi.

She looked back at me, happy that we were doing this together, but also still confused at what was going on. I grabbed her hands and just dove in. "I love you. I don't say it enough. I'm probably harder on you than I am to the boys, and that's not fair. I don't know why I'm like that, but I'll try to be better, more kind."

Medi smiled, and then something faltered in her eyes, "I love you too, and thank you for saying that."

She looked confused, opening her mouth but closing it without a question. I went ahead and took the moment and kept talking, just glad I got to say the first bit out loud. It was something I needed to say, something I'd been realizing as of late.

"I don't know how much you remember from last night. So I'm just going to pretend we're starting back at zero." I took a deep breath. I couldn't tell from her eyes if she was lost or just letting me say my piece. I got nervous and let go of her hands, and looked up at the night. I recognized the constellation Orion, but shook off the stars, needing to stay here on Earth. "So I guess everyone seems to know. That said, part of me really hopes this isn't a surprise, but I have to say something, and I have to say something now."

"Okay, say it, you're scaring me."

"I'm in love with Henry. I have no idea where it started, maybe when I was eleven and I saw him at the batting cages. Though it could have been when I was fourteen and he was at the zoo carrying around a baby duck. There have been a lot of these types of moments. I could write you a list, the kiddie crush stuff from when he was your boyfriend, and the big friendship emotions that come from seeing him every day and turned into so much more, but I don't want to hurt you. The two of you were together for so long, and I'm sure you loved him-"

"I didn't just love him, Lynman. I still do, but not in the same way I love Milo. I love Henry like family and all I want is for him to be happy. I want you both to be happy. If this is you asking for my blessing, which by the way you don't need to do, but if that pushes you," Medi said, "well then of course."

She pulled me into a tight hug. "I guess you're not a kid anymore."

I pulled back and away, "Did you hear that Llew? We're adults."

"Grown-ups!," Llew shouted, punching his fist into the sky.

"I wouldn't go that far," Abe added.

I hugged her once more.

When we finally came apart she said, "So, what are you waiting for, Lynman? Go get your man."

"Come on," I led the way into Henry's yard. "Well, the thing is. I do need a little help. It was sort of a dick move, me leaving like that the other morning, out the window-"

"I'm sorry, you left out the window the other morning? What morning was this?" Abe said, turning around with a frown and causing me to hop by him.

"Don't worry, I was high as a kite, old man prude," I said.

Llew laughed.

Abe shook his head.

"Grownups," he said looking at Medi, who was smiling watching all of this play out.

"What else did I miss this week?" asked Medi.

Llew and I looked at each other and couldn't help but laugh again.

"Will you tell her the other part when I'm gone," I said.

"What secret was that?" said Llew quizzically, "Oh the fact that you found out that Abe's your dad."

"Oh shit," said Medi and this time she actually looked shocked. She looked at Abe who shrugged.

"Yeah we talked about all this last night, don't you remember?" asked Llew.

"Really? I must have been so drunk," she said bewildered.

"It's hard being old, huh sis?" I said. "Anyway, that's old news, we're all good."

I clapped to make a point and capture their attention.

"Now if we can get back to the matter at hand, Henry." I gestured to the dark house. "I think maybe I should restart, so I've got to get up there, and well that's where you three come in."

"We were just in the garage, we couldn't have gotten the ladder?" asked Abe.

"The ladder," Llew scoffed, crossing his arms and shook his head.

"I came down without the ladder, I'm going back up the same way."

"Come on, just make a saddle," said Llew, and linked his fingers together to show Abe what he meant.

It was awkward with the wood pile, and Llew made sure to make all the comments he could about my weight. Medi added moral support, and direction. Finally, I shifted to Llew's shoulders, him being taller. I wasn't gentle because of his weight comments, but when I got to the window, I pushed and pushed and realized it wasn't going to budge.

"It's locked," I said.

"It's also pitch black in there," Medi added, moving to a side window and staring in.

"Yeah, I don't think he's here."

"Good, he won't see me drop you."

"Gentle Baby Joy," I said.

We spent a few moments shifting, dropping, catching and falling and I was back on the ground not much the worse for wear.

"Where could he be?" asked Medi.

"The guy has like a dozen jobs, he could be anywhere," said Llew.

"What day is it?" I asked not too sure anymore and tried to remember the things I knew and then it came to me and I waved off the question.

"Actually, I know where he is," I said.

What felt like a year ago, slid back as the beginning of the week and the start of this exhausting journey we were all on. It started with Henry asking me to the movies on Thursday. I knew he wouldn't expect me, but still he should be there doing his job.

"The movie theater."

"It's really late." Medi said.

"He'll be there." I was still nervous and I shrugged. "Well, I guess this I'll have to do on my own. I'll see you guys later."

"Looks like you got there," Abe said.

"What?"

"I knew you'd get there, get here, eventually," he kept on.

"Get where?" I demanded, still puzzled.

"This spot, this exact place. Dad knew it. He always said there would be a day when we would know the truth, and if we all loved each other enough, the rest of it would work itself out."

He smiled, we smiled the same toothy grin.

Llew listened to Abe and wiped away a tear that I found really unexpected. He caught me watching and hit me in the shoulder. "Go you jerk."

Medi hugged me. "Big emotional scene," she whispered and we laughed.

I walked backwards for a few steps, looking at the three of them, wanting to remember this moment and then turned heading into the cemetery.

I was unconsciously taking the long way. I wanted to stop by Mrs. Hayden's stone and I wanted a cigarette. I pulled the pack from my pocket and started packing it down.

"Hey Mrs. H," I whispered like I had so many times before. I'd told her so many secrets, so many stories, but I'd never told her this. "I've been a bit of an ass to your son lately. Maybe more than lately. I love him, whatever that means. It might not mean happily ever after. Maybe I screwed it up, or maybe it's just not right, but I have to stop lying and pretending. I promise I'll be good to him, better to him."

I stuck the cigarette in my mouth and went to light it, but I glanced up the hill and I saw a pile flowers that had been left behind earlier and I remembered it wasn't just Mrs. Hayden here any longer.

"Shit," I said and then whispered, "mouth."

Glancing back to Mrs. Hayden I was already walking uphill to where my dad had been laid to rest. "I guess we're not alone anymore. Talk later Mrs. H."

I held the cigarette in my closed fist and glanced away from the disturbed earth I had just seen earlier that day, but alone and in the dark I saw it for the first time. I stood next to Dad silently for a few moments breathing deep. I shook my head, and both laughed and scowled, opening both hands and seeing the cigarette and the lighter. A wave of knowledge pushed over me and I knew I wouldn't be smoking this cigarette and if I had my way, I'd already had my last.

"Fine," I muttered under my breath and added. "I heard you, you don't have to keep repeating yourself."

I started toward the trashcan on the path and tossed the lone smoke, the rest of the pack and the lighter.

"Are you happy?" I growled, but then swallowed hard, the frustration passed. False anger gone as quickly as it appeared. His memory was overwhelming.

"Are you happy?" I repeated, but with a different tone this time. There was no answer, but I didn't expect one.

"I love you Dad, and I miss you, but you don't have to worry. We're all going to be alright. I'll see you tomorrow."

I crossed out of the cemetery and onto the sidewalk toward town. I sped up, almost to a run. My feet searched out leaves to step on, to crunch like music announcing my passage. There were only a few leaves that had begun to fall. It had been a warm rainy summer and those leaves seemed to want to hang on the trees not wanting summer to end. I understood that. Change was hard. It was easier to hide in libraries, and behind books, to keep searching instead of invest in what is all around you. Like it or not, change happened, people died, people grew and leaves fell down to meet the ground where not far off seeds had given them life.

The theater should have been dark. It was closed by then, so the marquee should have been turned off. But what I saw stopped me in my tracks.

In red lettering it read, *Lycurgus "Curt" Newman, book seller, father, friend. You'll be missed, 1954-2019*

I stood there looking at the words, an announcement to shake the town. A man bigger than life, my father. It was hard to breathe. I looked all around wanting to see that I wasn't imagining this, there was no one out at that time of night, but still I knew this was real. Henry was real and so were his feelings. I went over to the side door that Henry always left open for me. There was a chance this time it would be locked, but I had to try.

I leaned lightly on the bar and it pushed open as my heart leapt. Most of the house lights were off, but a few still remained. I wasn't sure where Henry would be, but as I got deeper inside the theater I heard the sounds of the film escaping through open doors and saw the light of the movie setting down a path for me to follow.

It was a special film that was playing. An oldie but a goodie. I was happy that the town kids might get their first chance to see *The Princess Bride* and it would be up on the big screen.

Fifty foot tall Billy Crystal was doing his thing. Miracle Max was explaining about death. I let myself get caught up in the scene. I hadn't seen it in years, but I loved to think about it because of that night in the bar. The characters moved from talking about death to discussing true love, but Miracle Max wouldn't have any of that. A bit of an angry curmudgeon, Max corrected them, it wasn't true love, the nearly dead character said, but *to blave.*

"To blave?" I whispered. Now even more anchored to that memory of long ago. The memory of Henry waiting for me on the stairs. Waiting to see if I was alright, that I had made it home, then kissing me and mumbling something that could have been thanks, not mumbling, but saying what I now realized was a line from the movie.

"To blave," I repeated in shocked realization.

"Boo," said a voice behind me, "Booooo."

He was standing so close I felt his breath on my neck.

I turned around and saw Henry, he had found me and leaned back in the doorway. God, he could lean.

I smiled, the sort of smile held together by a million feelings trying to settle on one emotion but feeling all of them. There was a lot to say.

"The marquee, I can't say what that means to me. Thank you."

"It didn't seem right. I saw that obituary and it's hard to explain, but it didn't seem right."

"My dad wasn't someone you could fit Into twelve point font."

"No, he wasn't," Henry said and smiled.

I could have just stared at that smile and got lost in it, but I knew that was dangerous and maybe even cowardly and so I took the silence and made it my own.

"I shouldn't have ran off the other night. And I shouldn't have ran off or actually climbed out your window the next day. I was embarrassed and ashamed. I wanted to hide. My mom always says I run away from difficult situations. She said if I ran away from all the stuff this week, the funeral and my family I would regret it. She's right, and I am. I regret treating you like that. I'm always running, and I know I need to consider this stuff, not just with Dad and my family, but with other important and difficult moments in my life. And yet, the thing is, this shouldn't be difficult. I don't want to lose your friendship, but my god, I want more than just that. I shouldn't have kept my feelings inside so long. I should have listened to what you had to say the other night, even if it might not be what I wanted to hear. It's important for me to be present, and at least try to be honest. So say it, whatever you want to say, I'm here and I'll listen."

Henry heard what I said and nodded. He looked to the screen and then looked back at me while stepping forward, closing the space between us.

"It wasn't right," he said. Leaning in close, he swept a stray curl around my ear until there was no more space between us. "I wanted to be there for you. I needed to be there for you, but I didn't want to mix these days and these emotions. When I kiss you I don't want you thinking about what you've lost."

"When you kiss me?" I asked.

He made a noise of agreement, a sigh of want, and my knees went weak.

"What are you thinking about?" he asked.

Yet I didn't have an answer, there weren't words. In fact, it was hard to breathe. In his blue eyes I could see the reflection of the movie, a small square of light that was in focus and then gone and it was only him. Henry kissed me. There was not a worry or doubt in that kiss. I had no concern for what came next. No desire to be any place except this place. That's a promise. And you know, maybe even another puzzle piece had found its fit. That's the truth. It was an honest moment and so I kissed Henry back.

To Blave

www.ingramcontent.com/pod-product-compliance
Lightning Source LLC
Chambersburg PA
CBHW071127100726
47908CB00008B/2516